Praise for

"[An] oddball fairy tale . . . This s[ ] in the mind."

—*The New York Times*

"The novel is written in partial rhyme . . . [and] the singsong prose adds to the madcap nature of this lighthearted and yet sorrowful tale."

—*San Francisco Chronicle*

"A charming tale that revels in colorful detail and language and a heartrending depiction of the brutal march of mental illness. . . . A unique, evocative debut."

—*Kirkus Reviews*

"This fanciful love story, fraught with sadness, is a sweet meditation on the more unorthodox gifts that parents leave the children they cherish."

—*Publishers Weekly*

"Spirited and graciously zany, *Waiting for Bojangles* is a passionate love story told through the eyes of a child."

—*France-Amérique*

"Alternately delightful and melancholic."

"At once delightfully whimsical and hugely touching."

"A very well-written story, with a touch of craziness, an awesome rhythm, and a libertine use of words. I loved the book, I loved the subject. A wonderful mix of reality and invention. What a terrific book."

"Bourdeaut tells the story with incredible ease, without falling into the 'feel good' trap."

"A worthy heir of a tradition that includes authors such as Queneau, Prévert, and Romain Gary."

"In this novel, fantasy reigns supreme. The author plunges us into a delightful, joyful, and witty mess."

"This smart and memorable novel about a special family tells a universal story sure to leave an impact on the reader."

Waiting for Bojangles

A Novel

Olivier Bourdeaut

TRANSLATED BY REGAN KRAMER

SIMON & SCHUSTER PAPERBACKS

NEW YORK   LONDON   TORONTO   SYDNEY   NEW DELHI

Simon & Schuster Paperbacks
An Imprint of Simon & Schuster, Inc.
1230 Avenue of the Americas
New York, NY 10020

Copyright © 2015 by Éditions Finitude
English language translation copyright © 2019 by Regan Kramer
Originally published in France in 2015 by Éditions Finitude as
En Attendant Bojangles.

First Simon & Schuster paperback edition March 2020

SIMON & SCHUSTER PAPERBACKS and colophon are registered trademarks of Simon & Schuster, Inc.

For information about special discounts for bulk purchases, please contact Simon & Schuster Special Sales at 1-866-506-1949 or business@simonandschuster.com.

The Simon & Schuster Speakers Bureau can bring authors to your live event. For more information or to book an event, contact the Simon & Schuster Speakers Bureau at 1-866-248-3049 or visit our website at www.simonspeakers.com.

Interior design by Carly Loman

Manufactured in the United States of America

10 9 8 7 6 5 4 3 2 1

Library of Congress Cataloging-in-Publication Data is available.

ISBN 978-1-5011-4591-9
ISBN 978-1-5011-7509-1 (pbk)
ISBN 978-1-5011-4592-6 (ebook)

To my parents,
for that blend of patience and benevolence,
the daily proof of their endearments

Some people never go crazy.
What truly horrible lives they must lead.

Charles Bukowski

This is my true story,
with lies going backward and forward,
because life is often like that.

1.

My father told me that before I was born, he hunted flies with a harpoon for a living. He showed me the harpoon and a dead fly. "I quit because it was very hard work and very poorly rewarded," he explained as he packed the tools of his former trade back into a lacquered box. "Now I open garages. It's a lot of work, but it's very well rewarded."

During the first period of the first day of school, when everyone introduces themselves, I spoke, with no small amount of pride, about my father's professions, but all it got me was some gentle scolding and copious teasing. "The truth is poorly rewarded, when for once it was as entertaining as a lie," I lamented. My father was actually a man of the law. "The law puts food on our table!" he guffawed as he filled his pipe.

He was neither a judge, nor a legislator, nor a debt collector, nor a lawyer—nothing like that. Thanks to inside information about the provisions of a new law, he was the first person to step into a new profession created out of thin air by the Senator. And that's how my father became a "garage opener." New rules mean new jobs. To make sure the nation's fleet of cars was safe and sound, the Senator decreed that everyone would have to pass inspection. Owners of jalopies, limousines, vans, and rattletraps alike had to take their vehicles for a checkup to avoid accidents. Rich or poor, everyone had to do it. Since it was mandatory, he inevitably charged a lot for it, a small fortune. He charged for entering and for exiting, for the initial inspection and the follow-ups, and judging by his laughter, that was fine with him. "I'm saving lives, I'm saving lives!" he'd chuckle, as he flipped through his bank statements.

Back then, saving lives paid very well. After he opened a lot of garages, he sold them to the competition, which was a relief for Mom. She didn't really care for his saving lives, because it meant he worked so much that we hardly ever saw him. "I'm working late so I can stop early," he'd reply, which I didn't really understand. I often didn't understand my father. I did a little more as the years went by, but never completely. Which was fine with me.

He had told me he was born that way, but when I was still pretty young, I realized that the ashy, slightly swollen indentation on the right side of his lower lip, which gave him a nice, somewhat twisted smile, was actually due to diligent pipe smoking. His hairstyle—parted in the middle with little waves on either side—reminded me of the Prussian cavalry officer in the painting in the front hall. Aside from the two of them, I'd never seen anyone whose hair looked like that. His slightly hollow eye sockets and lightly bulging blue eyes gave him a curious gaze, deep and wise. Back then, I only ever saw him happy, and in fact, he often used to say, "I'm a happy fool!" To which my mother would reply, "We'll take your word for it, George, we'll take your word for it!"

He would hum, badly, all the time. Sometimes he'd whistle, just as badly, but like anything that's done cheerfully, it was bearable. He told great stories, and on those rare evenings when we didn't have any company, he would fold his tall, lean body onto my bed for a bedtime story. He'd begin with a grin, then his tale of a jinn, a leprechaun, a twin or a peppercorn would chase all my sleepiness away. Things usually wound up with me jumping up and down with excitement on my bed, or hiding, terrified, behind the curtains. "That's a very tall story for such a little boy," he would say as he slipped out of my room. And once again, you could take his word for it.

On Sundays, to make up for the week's excesses, he would pump iron. Standing in front of the big mirror with its fancy gilt frame topped with a majestic bow, he would strip to the waist and, pipe in mouth, lift tiny little barbells while listening to jazz music. He called that his "gym & tonic" because he'd pause to gulp a gin & tonic and tell my mother, "You should get some exercise, Miss Daisy, I'm telling you, it's fun, and you feel great afterward!"

To which my mother, who was trying—one eye closed, tongue sticking out in concentration—to spear the olive in her martini with the little paper parasol, would reply, "You should try orange juice, George. I swear that exercise wouldn't be nearly as much fun with OJ instead of G & T. And would you be so kind, monsieur, as to cease calling me Daisy forthwith? Pick another name, or else I'm going to start mooing like a heifer!"

I never really understood why, but my father never called my mother by the same name for more than a day or two in a row. Even though she tired of some names sooner than others, she loved the ritual, and every morning in the kitchen, I could see her watching my father with excited anticipation, holding her coffee cup or her chin in her hands as she awaited the verdict. "Oh no, you wouldn't do that to me! Not Renee,

not today! We've got company coming for dinner tonight!"
she would giggle. Then she'd turn to the mirror and greet the
new Renee with a pout, the new Josephine with a regal gaze,
the new Marylou with puffed-out cheeks. "Besides, there's
absolutely nothing Renee-like about my wardrobe!"

There was just one day a year when my mother
always had the same name: on February 15, her name
was Georgette. It still wasn't her real name, but Saint
Georgette's Day was the day after Saint Valentine's Day.
My parents didn't think it was very romantic to be seated
at a table in a restaurant filled with mandatory, predictable
professions of love on Valentine's Day. So each year, they
would celebrate on Saint Georgette's Day, and enjoy an almost empty restaurant with the staff dancing attendance
on them alone. Besides, Dad thought that a romantic festiv-
ity had to have a woman's name. "Please reserve your best
table in the name of George and Georgette. And can you
promise me that you don't have any of those awful heart-
shaped desserts left? None? Thank the Lord!" he would say
as he booked a table at a fancy restaurant. For them, Saint
Georgette's was no time to act like marionettes.

After the business with the garages, my father didn't have
to get up in the morning to put food on the table any-

more, so he started writing books. All the time. A lot of them. He would sit at his big desk, writing, laughing as he wrote, writing down what made him laugh, filling his pipe, the ashtray and the room with smoke and the paper with ink, while emptying cups of coffee and whole bottles of mixed drinks. But the publishers' replies were all the same: "It's clever and well written, but we can make neither heads nor tails of it." To cheer him up after the rejections, my mother would say, "Why would anyone want to make heads or tails out of a book? What a strange idea!" That always cracked us up.

My father used to say that Mom was on a first-name basis with the stars in the sky, which seemed strange, because my mother never called anyone by their first name—not even me. Nor did my mother ever call our pet demoiselle crane by a pet name. The elegant and surprising bird lived in our apartment, parading her undulating long black neck, white plumes jutting from her violently red eyes. My parents had brought her back from a journey to I-don't-know-where, from their life before me.

We called her Mademoiselle Superfluous, because she served no purpose, except for squawking loudly for no reason at every season, leaving round pyramids on the parquet floor, and waking me up in the middle of the night by tap-tap-tapping on my bedroom door. Like my father's stories, Mademoiselle was very tall, even with her head tucked under her wing to sleep. As I child, I used to try to copy her, but it was pretty tricky.

Mademoiselle loved when Mom would lie on the couch to read and pet her head for hours on end. Like all wise birds, Mademoiselle loved reading. One day my mother decided to take Mademoiselle Superfluous shopping in town. She made her a lovely pearl leash, but Mademoiselle was so spooked by the sight of all those people—and so many people were spooked by the sight of Mademoiselle—that she squawked louder than ever. An old lady with a dachshund even said that it was inhuman and dangerous to walk a bird down the street on a leash. "Feathers or fur, what difference does it make?" Mom asked. "Mademoiselle has never bitten anyone, and it seems to me that she's far more elegant than your fuzzy hot dog! Come, Mademoiselle Superfluous, let's go home; people here are so discourteous!"

Mom got home in high dudgeon that day. When she was in that state, she would find my father to relate the whole story to him in great detail. She wouldn't go back to being her usual jovial self until after she'd finished.

She got upset easily, but my father would resolve things breezily. His voice was very soothing to her. The rest of the time, she was rapturous about everything, found the world's progress thrilling, and skipped along with it joyfully.

She didn't treat me like an adult, or like a child, more like a character from a book that she loved very dearly, and that could absorb all her attention in an instant. She never wanted to hear about trials or tribulations. "When reality is sad or mundane, make up a lovely story, young man," she would say. "You tell such beautiful falsehoods, it would be such a shame to deprive us." So I would make up a story about my day, and when I was done, she would clap her hands and giggle, "What a fabulous day, my darling son, what a day. I'm so happy for you, young man, you must have had such a wonderful time!" Then she would hug me tight and kiss me. She was nibbling me, she would say. I loved when she nibbled me. Every morning, after receiving her daily name, she would give me one of her freshly scented gloves, so that her hand could guide me all day long.

"Some of her features bore traces of her childlike manner: apple cheeks and green eyes that sparkled with mischief. The

shimmering barrettes she used to tame her lioness's mane granted her the elfin sassiness of a late-blooming Plain Jane. But her bee-stung crimson lips miraculously held her precariously perched slim white cigarettes, and her long eyelashes, measuring the world up, showed the beholder that she had grown up. Her outfits, slightly extravagant and extremely elegant—at least in how they were put together—proved to observant eyes that she had lived, had known some stormy weather."

That's what my father had written in a secret notebook that I read later, afterward. While it may not have had a tail, it definitely had a head.

My parents danced all the time, and all over the place. With their friends in the evening; just the two of them morning, noon and night. Sometimes I danced with them. They were totally footloose and fancy-free, knocking over anything in their path, my father flinging my mother into space, catching her by her fingernails after a pirouette or two, or even three. He would swing her between his legs, twirl her around him like a weather vane, and when he accidentally let her slip from his grasp, Mom would wind up plopped on the floor with her dress fanned out around her like a teacup on a saucer.

When they danced, they would shake up amazing cocktails, with paper umbrellas, olives, spoons and whole collections of bottles. On the living-room couch, in front of a huge black-and-white snapshot of Mom diving into a pool in an evening gown, there was a lovely old-fashioned turntable that always played the same Nina Simone album, and the same song: "Mr. Bojangles." It was the only record that was allowed to turn on that table; all other music had to settle for a newer, drabber stereo. The song was truly crazy, happy and sad at the same time, and it would put my mother in the same mood. It lasted a long time, but always ended too soon, and my mother would clap her hands excitedly and shout, "Let's play 'Bojangles' again!" Then you had to grasp the arm and set the diamond needle back on the edge. Only a diamond could produce music like that.

Our apartment was very big, so that we could have lots and lots of company. The front hall was tiled with big black-and-white squares that formed a huge checkerboard. My father bought forty black and white cushions, and after school, we would have gigantic checkers parties under the watchful eye of the Prussian cavalier. He was the referee, but he never said anything. Sometimes Mademoiselle Superfluous disrupted the game, pushing the white cushions around with her head or stabbing them with her beak. Only the white ones; we didn't know if it was because she didn't like them or because she loved them too much. We never did find out. Like everyone, Mademoiselle had her secrets.

In one corner of the hall, there was a mountain of mail that my parents had tossed on the floor unopened. The mountain was so huge that I could toss myself onto it without getting hurt. Warm and welcoming, it was part of the furniture. Sometimes my father would say, "If you're a bad boy, you're going to have to open all that mail and sort it!" But he never made me do it; he didn't have a mean bone in his body.

The living room was a real madhouse. There were two bloodred club chairs for my parents to sit and drink in; a glass table filled with sand of every color; and a huge blue couch that was very plump and meant to be jumped on: my mother recommended it highly. Sometimes she would jump with me. I would cheer when she jumped so high that she touched the glittering crystal chandelier. My father was right: if she wanted to, she really could call the stars by their first names.

Facing the couch, resting on an old trunk covered with stickers from cities around the world, was a musty old television set that didn't work very well. All the channels showed images of anthills in gray, black and white. To punish the TV for its poor programming, my father made it wear a dunce cap. Sometimes he would warn me, "If you're a bad boy, I'll turn the television on!" Watching that television for hours was torture. But he hardly ever did it; he really didn't have a mean bone in his body.

On the hutch, which she hated, my mother grew ivy, which she loved. Before long, the hutch had turned into a giant plant, furniture that lost its leaves and needed watering. It was a funny piece of furniture, a funny plant. In the dining room, there was everything you needed: a big table and lots of chairs for company, and for us, too, of course, which was the least you would expect.

Leading to the bedrooms was the long hall where we broke speed records. The stopwatch said my father always won and Mademoiselle Superfluous lost; she wasn't too keen on competition, and besides, the noise of applause scared her. My room had three beds: a little one, a medium one, and a big one. I had chosen to keep my beds from when I was little, because I had good memories in them. I saw it as an embarrassment of riches even if Dad thought that my riches looked like a dump.

There was a poster of the French pop singer Claude

François in a rhinestone-studded outfit on the wall. Dad had drawn a target onto the poster to turn it into a dartboard. He said that Claude François sang like a strangled cat, but that fortunately, the electric company had put a stop to all that.* I didn't really understand how or why, or if it was the truth or a lie. Because the real truth is, my father was hard to understand sometimes.

The kitchen floor was cluttered with all sorts of potted herbs for cooking, but most of the time Mom forgot to water them, so there was hay everywhere. On the rare days that she did water them, she would overdo it. The pots leaked like sieves, and the kitchen turned into a skating rink. It was a huge mess that lasted until the soil in the pots soaked up the excess. Mademoiselle Superfluous loved when the kitchen was flooded. She would flap her wings and puff her neck out happily. It reminded her of her old life, Mom said affably.

Hanging from the ceiling amidst the pots and pans was a dried pig trotter that looked disgusting but tasted delicious. While I was at school, Mom would make lots of good

---

* Claude François died in 1978 of accidental electrocution in his bathtub.

things to eat that she gave to a catering service to bring back when we needed them; our guests were always very impressed. The fridge was too small for so many people, so it was always empty. Mom would invite tons of people over to eat, at any time of day: friends, certain neighbors (the ones who didn't mind noise), my father's former colleagues, the concierge, her husband, the mailman (when he showed up at the right time), the grocery-store owner who came from faraway North Africa but whose shop was right downstairs, and once, even an old man in a ragged shirt and baggy pants who smelled awful but who seemed pleased to be there.

Mom had no time for clocks, so sometimes when I came home from school there was roast lamb ready to snack on, and other times I had to wait until the middle of the night for dinner. In the meantime, we danced and munched olives. Occasionally we danced so much we couldn't eat, so late at night, Mother would cry to let me know she was really sorry. Then she'd nibble me and hug me to her wet face and cocktail smell. That's just how my mother was, which was fine with me.

Our guests laughed long and hard, and from time to time, when they were tired out from having laughed so much they would spend the night on one of my beds. In the morning, Mademoiselle Superfluous, who was not really in favor of sleeping in, would wake them with her squawking. When there was company, I always slept in my biggest bed, so that when I woke up, I would see them folded up like accordions in my baby beds, which made me laugh my head off.

Three nights a week, we had the same guest, who had his own room at our place: the Senator, who would come up from his region in the center of France to take his seat in Parliament. My father affectionately called him "the Creep." I never did find out how they'd met—the story changed with every cocktail—but they were always as thick as thieves.

The Creep had an angled haircut—not a fancy one, like a girl's, but a crew cut with right angles—on top of a round, red face divided by a bushy moustache, and thin steel-framed glasses looped over strange shrimp-shaped ears. He explained to me that rugby did that to your ears after a few years. I didn't really understand how, but in any case, I decided that "gym & tonic" was less dangerous than rugby, at least for your ears. The color, the texture, the crushed cartilage . . . they really looked just like shrimp. That's just how it was, but he didn't seem to mind.

When he laughed, the Creep's body shook with spasms,

and since he laughed all the time, his shoulders had a permanent tremor. His voice was loud, and it crackled like an old transistor. He always had an enormous cigar that he never lit. He'd have it in his hand or his mouth when he arrived, and he'd slip it into a case when he left. As soon he crossed our threshold, he'd start shouting, "Caipiroska, Caipiroska!"

I used to think he was calling for his Russian girlfriend. Since she was never there, my father would serve him a frosty cocktail with mint to cheer him up, and that always seemed to do the trick. My mother liked the Creep because he was funny, because he rained compliments on her and because he had helped us earn heaps of money, and I liked him for exactly the same reasons, no more, no less.

At our parties, he would try to kiss all of my mother's friends. My father said he would jump at any chance he got. Sometimes it worked, and he would go jump his chances in his room. A few minutes later, he'd come back out, redder than ever, shouting for his Russian girlfriend, because he must have realized that something wasn't right. "Caipiroska! Caipiroska!" he'd bellow gleefully, as he hooked his glasses back over his shrimp ears.

During the day, he'd go to work at the Luxembourg Palace, which was in Paris, for some reason I could never really understand. He would say he was going to work late, but he always came back pretty early. The Senator had a strange lifestyle. When he came back from work, he'd say that his job had been a lot more interesting before the wall came down, because you could see things more clearly.

I figured he meant that they'd done construction work in his office, and that they must have knocked down a wall and used the stones to block some windows. So it made sense that he left work early, because no one would want to work in conditions like that, not even a creep. Dad would say, "The Creep is my dearest friend, because his friendship is priceless!" That I understood perfectly.

With the garage money, Dad had purchased a beautiful castle in the air. It was in Spain, far south of Paris. You had to drive a little, fly a little, drive a little more, and be very patient. Perched on a mountainside, floating above an all-white village where the streets were empty in the afternoon and full of people at night, all you could see from the castle was pine forests. Well, practically all. In a corner on the right, there were terraced groves with rows of olive, orange and almond trees dropping all the way down to the shore of a milky-blue lake formed by a magnificent dam. Dad told me that he had built the dam himself, and that if it weren't for him, all the water would have run away. I wasn't sure I believed him: there weren't any tools in the house, and I'm nobody's fool.

The seashore wasn't far off, and the beaches, apartment buildings, restaurants and traffic jams were jam-packed with people. Mom said she couldn't understand why people would exchange one crowded place for another on vacation. She said that the beaches were fouled with the grease that people slathered on their skin to tan, even though they were already fat and greasy without it. But that didn't keep us from sunbathing on the pint-size beaches around our lake. With just enough room for three beach towels, they were perfect for us, and never foul.

On the roof of the castle there was a big terrace with wispy clouds of jasmine. Unlike the crowds on the beaches, the jasmine smelled really nice. The view was so spectacular that it made my parents thirsty, so they drank wine with pieces of fruit in it. We ate tons of fruit by day, and drank it as we danced at night. "Mr. Bojangles" came with us, of course, and Mademoiselle Superfluous joined us a little later; we had to go pick her up at the airport, because she had a special status. She traveled in a box with a hole for her long neck to stick out of, so of course she squawked her little head off, with good reason for once. My parents would invite all their friends to come and eat fruit, dance and sunbathe at their castle in the air. They all said it was absolutely heavenly, and we had no reason to think any differently. Whenever I wanted to go to heaven, I could, but usually we went when my parents decided we should.

Mom used to love to tell me the story of Mr. Bojangles. His story was like his song: lovely, melancholy and nice and long. That's why my parents loved slow-dancing to it. It had feeling, and it went on and on. Mr. Bojangles lived in New Orleans, although it was a really long time ago. He used to travel with his dog and his ragged shirt and baggy pants. But his dog up and died, he up and died, and Bojangles cried and cried. Then he had to dance with just his ragged shirt and baggy pants. He'd dance at honky-tonks, minstrel shows and county fairs; Mr. Bojangles danced all the time and everywhere, just like my parents. People gave him drinks and tips, so he'd dance for them in his worn-out shoes; he'd jump so high, he'd jump so high and he'd lightly touch down. Mom said he danced to bring his dog back, she'd heard it from someone who knew. As for her, well, she danced to bring Mr. Bojangles back. That was why she danced all the time. To bring him back, that's all.

2.

"*Call me what you will! But please, entertain me, conjure up stardom. Everybody here has sprayed themselves with boredom!*" *she said theatrically, as she snatched two glasses of champagne from the buffet. "The only reason I'm here at all is to find myself a life-insurance policy," she declared emphatically, before knocking back the first glass in a single gulp, her slightly wild eyes plunging straight into mine. And as I reached for the glass I naively believed was intended for me, she downed it as quickly as she had the first. Then she looked me up and down, stroking her chin, informing me with a laugh and a saucy grin, "And you are assuredly the best-looking policy I've seen at this god-awful gala!" Common sense should have urged me to flee her siren call. For that matter, I never should have met her at all.*

To celebrate the opening of my tenth garage, my banker had invited me to a two-day-long cocktail party at a five-star hotel on the Riviera. The event was called a "success week-end" but it was really just a seminar for up-and-coming young entrepreneurs. In addition to the absurd name, there were lots of morose people and all sorts of workshops run by fleabag experts with faces worn down by knowledge and data.

Ever since I was a child visiting friends' houses, I would pass the time by dreaming up wild tales about myself to entertain my companions. At dinner the first night, I served up my family's lineage right from the first course: I was descended from a Hungarian prince whose distant ancestor had been a close friend of Count Dracula. "Contrary to what they have tried to make us believe ever since, he was actually a man of rare courtesy, a real prince! I have in my home certain documents which prove that the poor gentleman was the victim of a terrible smear campaign, as many other noblemen were, explicably, despicably jealous of him."

Now, in situations like that, you always have to ignore the skeptical glances and stay as focused as a shark on the most gullible people at the table. You overwhelm them with minute details until they take the bait and make a remark that confirms your fable. On the night in question, the wife of a wine grower from Bordeaux nodded her head and declared, "I knew it! That story always struck me as being a bit much, too ghastly to be true! It's a myth!" She was followed by her husband, who brought everyone else along, and that was all anyone talked about for the rest of dinner. Everyone shared their own wisdom, the doubts they'd always had. They convinced themselves and each other that what I'd said was true, spinning an entire scenario from my initial falsehood. By the end of the meal, no one would have dared to confess that they had ever believed, even for a moment, in the story of Count Dracula the Impaler, which happens to be true.

Giddy with success, I committed a new offense with a different set of marks at lunch the next day. This time, I was the son of a rich American carmaker with automotive plants in Detroit, who had grown up within earshot of the racket of the assembly line. I raised the stakes by saddling myself with a severe case of autism that had kept me speechless until the age of seven. Winning hearts through compulsive lying that plucks at your victims' heartstrings really is the easiest thing in the world to do.

"But what could your first word possibly have been?" the woman on my right wondered out loud.

"Tire," I answered, looking proud.

"Tire?!" my dining companions echoed in unison.

"Yes, tire," I said once again.

"It's amazing, isn't it? So that's why you own so many garages. It figures. Life really is crazy sometimes," my neighbor said, staring into space with a sigh. Her untouched plate was spirited back to the kitchen by and by. The rest of the lunch chatter was devoted to life's little coincidences, people's fates, and how their heritage can color their whole existences. I was basking in the almond cognac and the crazy, selfish pleasure of briefly monopolizing a group's attention with stories as sturdy as the wind.

But I digress. I was about to take my leave from that charming assembly—before my madcap tales crashed into each other at the Flailing Wall, by the pool where the whole group was supposed to meet up for a mini society ball—when a young woman in a feathered cap and gossamer dress began to dance with great finesse. She held a long slim cigarette in one gloved hand, and while her other hand whipped her sheer white shawl into a frenzy of movements that a living breathing partner might have envied, I remained fascinated by the undulations of her body, the cadence that made the feathers in her headdress endlessly sway and swish, like one of those wheels Tibetans use to pray with. Shifting with the rhythm from the regal grace of a swan to the swift precision of a raptor, she had me nailed to the spot: I feared I had met my captor.

I assumed that she was being paid to entertain the guests and enliven an otherwise mundane event. Like a Roaring

Twenties floozy and a Cheyenne on peyote rolled into one, she skipped from group to group, grabbing the men's hands without so much as a howdy-do, spinning them 'til they were dizzy, throwing their spouses into a tizzy. Then without further ado, she'd fling them back to their sad lives and the bitter gaze of their jealous wives. I don't know quite how long I had been standing there under the grape arbor, smoking my pipe and downing the glasses the waiters brought with swiftness and ardor. I was already at least two sheets to the wind when her gaze came to rest on my shy, glazed-over eyes, and I was pinned. Hers were the exact shade of celadon, deep enough to drown every shred of wit I could claim, causing me to stutter out a phrase that was tragically mundane: "What's your name?"

"Do you know I've got a painting of a handsome Prussian cavalry officer hanging over the mantel at home?" she replied. "Believe it or not, your haircut is just like his! I have met everyone in the world, and I can assure you that no one, absolutely no one, has had a haircut like that since World War I! Where have you been getting your hair done since Prussia ceased to exist?"

"My hair doesn't grow. It never has. Since you asked, I can tell you that I was born with this dratted haircut several centuries ago by now. As a child, I looked like an old man, but as

time goes by, my haircut is starting to suit my age. I'm counting on fashion's way of making everything old be new again
to send me to my grave looking up-to-date!"

"I'm serious! You, my dear, are the exact doppelganger of
that Prussian cavalier. I've been madly in love with him since
I was a child, and I've married him a thousand times by now.
Since your wedding day is the happiest day of your life, we decided to get married every day, to make our lives a perpetual
paradise."

"Now that you mention it, I do vaguely remember a mili-
tary campaign when I was in the cavalry lines. I had my por-
trait painted after a battle crowned with success. I'm thrilled
to learn that I now live over your mantel and have married
you a thousand times."

"You can laugh all you want, but I swear it's true! For
reasons you can easily construe, the marriage has never been
consummated; I'm still a virgin, though it's a bit outdated. It's
not for want of dancing in the nude before the fireplace, but
my poor horseman seems to be something of a prude, despite
his fierce warrior's face!"

"I'm stunned. I would have thought that your sensual
grace could raise an entire army! Your soldier must be a eu-
nuch. But tell me, where did you learn to trip the light so fan-
tastically, and in such a tunic?"

"*This is terribly awkward. I have yet another shocking confession, one that's truly wild. Believe it or not, dear friend, but my father was Josephine Baker's secret love child!*"

"*By Jove, this is incredible! Josephine Baker was a close friend of mine before. We stayed at the same hotel in Paris during the war.*"

"*Don't tell me that you and Josephine . . . !? Hmm, you know what I mean.*"

"*Well, actually, she did come to my room when the bombs were dropping one warm summer's night. What with the fear, the heat and the closeness, it simply felt right.*"

"*Sweet Jesus, then you might be my grandfather! Let's have heaps of drinks to celebrate our finding each other!*" *she proposed while, I should mention, waving her hands to attract a waiter's attention.*

We spent the entire afternoon in that spot near the woods, twittering like goldfinches, shifting only a few inches, outdoing each other's nonsense and silly theories, feigning belief in each other's stories. Behind her I saw the sun begin its ineluctable path toward setting—it even crowned her for a fleeting moment before dropping behind the rocks, gracing us with the halo of its celestial netting. Having reached out repeatedly, and in growing misery, for the glasses of champagne I still thought were meant for me, I finally became resigned to her custom. Since it required taking two glasses in one fell swoop, I started ordering my scotch on the rocks by the pair as well. That breakneck pace soon led to her subjecting me to an inverted questionnaire: she would inform me as matter-of-factly as could be of the praise she was craving, then tack a question tag onto the end of the phrase she was waving. "You're thrilled to meet me, aren't you?" *or* "I would make a wonderful spouse, wouldn't I?" *and then she added,* "I'm sure you're wondering if I'm out of your league, am I right? But don't torture yourself, my dear, you have me intrigued, so I'm on sale until midnight tonight. Don't miss your chance!" *she announced, shimmying her bosom to make it dance.*

I had arrived at that peculiar moment when you can still choose, still choose your future feelings. I was perched at the top of the slide. It wasn't too late to decide to scurry back down the ladder, hurry away before I had her. I could find a flimsy pretext to flee the whimsy of our context. Or I could let go, swing my legs over and let gravity take over, bask in the heady feeling of not being able to stop, of losing control, of steering my life toward a shining unknown goal, like sinking into a box of soft golden quicksand.

I could see perfectly well that she wasn't all there, that

her delirious green eyes hid secret fault lines, and I ought to
beware. That her plump, childish cheeks concealed a painful
past, and that this beautiful young woman, who at first glance
was droll and dazzling, had been through the mill and had
emerged bruised and unraveling. I was thinking that that had
to be why she danced so madly—both gladly and sadly—to
forget her troubles, that's all.

Stupidly, I was thinking that my professional life had been
crowned with success, that I was almost rich and fairly good-
looking, right? So I could easily find myself a normal wife, have
a quiet life: a drink before dinner and lights out by midnight.
I was thinking that I was already a bit of a loon, so perhaps
it wasn't such a good idea for me to fall for a complete loony
tune; that like a single amputee dating a double, our pairing
would necessarily lead us into trouble. In a word, I was starting to cave like a coward. While she flickered like a flame, tossing her mane, my shoulders were stooped. The prospect of an
inscrutable life, rife with incomputable strife, had me spooked.

And then, at the first notes of a jazzy tune, she tossed her
gauzy shawl, as pale as the moon, around my neck, yanking me
toward her with a gesture neither weak nor meek, and we found
ourselves dancing cheek to cheek. Into her eyes I looked, and I
knew right away I was hooked. I had been mulling a question
that was already settled: I belonged to that lovely green-eyed

lady. I had swung my legs up and over and was sliding into the
mist, without having realized it, before we'd even kissed.

"Nature calls, I'm bursting from all that drink. Wait here,
don't move, don't breathe, don't even blink!" she begged me,
fiddling her long pearl necklace nervously, while her knees
knocked impatiently at the door of this emergency.

"Why would I move? I haven't been in a better place since
I can't remember when!" I reassured her, with one hand sig-
naling a waiter to quench my thirst yet again.

As I watched her head toward the ladies' room, with
hurried but happy steps, I found myself face-to-face with my
neighbor from lunch, one of the sales reps. Furious, drunk and
out of control, she wagged a threatening finger at me, trying to
inspire fear. "So you know Dracula, do you?" she shrieked, as
the others drew near.

"Well, not exactly," I answered, caught completely off
guard.

"You're an autist and a prince! You're from Hungary and
the USA! You're nuts! Why did you lie to us?" she screamed
as I started backing away from her fuss, feeling unredeemed.

"This guy's a sicko, he should be tarred and feathered!"
a man in the crowd shouted in a voice that was weathered.

"It's not incompatible," I muttered, stuck in the cul-de-sac of my falsehoods, like a deer caught in the woods. Then, know-ing that my back was to the wall, I burst out in liberating laughter, no longer caring at all.

"He really is nuts, he's still laughing at us!" my accuser pointed out correctly, as she kept stalking toward me.

"All right, I went off the rails, but you didn't have to be-lieve my tales; I took a gamble, we had fun; the upshot is, you lost, and I won!" I replied, backing dangerously close to the pool, looking like a fool, with a glass of whiskey in each hand.

I was teetering at the edge when my accuser abruptly lifted off, took flight, then—crash! She fell into the glittering water, making a huge splash.

"I beg you NOT to excuse me: I simply couldn't resist! This man is my grandfather, Josephine Baker's lover, a Prus-sian horseman and my future husband, all rolled into one, and I adore him. That was no passing whim—I'd do anything for him!"

In the blink of a cocktail, the whirl of a dance, she twirled me in her veil, I didn't stand a chance. That flighty woman filled my whole soul with gladness by inviting me to share her madness.

9.

At school, nothing went as planned, and I mean *nothing*, especially not for me. When I described what went on at home, the teacher didn't believe me, and my classmates didn't either. So I started lying backward. It served the general interest, and especially my own. At school, I had a normal mother; "Mr. Bojangles" was just some record that spun like any other; Mom's name was always the same; Mademoiselle Superfluous had never heard of us; the Creep wasn't a famous senator, just an obscure inventor, and I had dinner at dinnertime, like everybody else. It was better that way. I lied forward at home and backward at school; it was complicated for me, but simpler for everybody else.

Lies weren't the only thing I did backward. My writing went that way, too. I wrote "like a mirror," the teacher said, even though I knew perfectly well that mirrors couldn't write. The teacher lied sometimes, too, but it seems that she was allowed to. Everybody could tell little white lies, because in terms of tranquility, they were better than the truth, the whole truth and nothing but the truth. My mother loved my mirror writing though, so when I got home from school, she would ask me to write whatever popped into my head: prose, shopping lists, mushy love poems. "That's wonderful, write my name of the day in mirror writing so I can see it!" she'd say, urging me on, her eyes bright with admiration beyond measure. She kept the slips of paper in a jewelry box, because, she said, "writing like that is worth its weight in gold, a real treasure!"

To make me write right, the teacher sent me to a lady who could straighten letters out without even touching them. She could fix them without any tools, and make them go the right way. So, to Mom's misfortune, I was almost cured. I say "almost," because on top of everything else, I was left-handed, but the teacher couldn't do anything about that. She said that fate really had it in for me, but that's just how it was. Before I was born, she added, they used to strap kids' wrong arms to their chests to cure them, but that kind of treatment was over now. Sometimes her lies made me furrow my brow.

The teacher had a lovely, sandy-colored permanent, as though a desert storm were always blowing on her head.

I thought it was beautiful. She also had a bump in her sleeve. At first I thought it was a disease, but one fine day when the weather was bad and she had a cold, I saw her take the bump out and blow her nose in it. I thought that was quite impulsive, and more than a little repulsive.

Mother didn't get along with Desert Storm in the least, because of my writing, of course, but also because my teacher never wanted to let me go to heaven when my parents had decided to. She wanted us to wait until school vacation, like everybody else. She said that what with my writing issue, I was already behind, and if I kept missing school, I was going to miss a lot of boats, too.

"The almond trees are in bloom right now," my mother would explain. "Surely you don't mean for my son to miss the almond trees! It's the loveliest way to mark the end of winter. If you make him miss it, you're going to throw his aesthetic balance all off-kilter!" Manifestly, the teacher cared about neither almond trees nor their blooms, and she didn't give a damn about my aesthetic balance either, but we used to go to heaven anyway. It would throw the teacher into a terrible rage, and sometimes her bad mood would last until I got back. So I tried not to be rude, and I sat at the back of the room when I could.

I really didn't know how to apologize to the teacher

for my mirror writing, the almond trees and the heavenly vacations any time of year, so one day I decided to do her a favor. You see, all sorts of bad stuff used to happen in the classroom when she had her back turned to us and the rest of her facing the board. Since she didn't have eyes in the back of her head, I decided I could be an extra pair of eyes for her. So I told on everyone, about everything, every day. The spitballers, the chatterers and cheaters, the glue-game players, funny-face makers and candy eaters.

What a commotion it caused the first time! Absolutely no one was expecting it, so there was an embarrassing silence. The teacher gave the spitballers detention and completely forgot to thank me. The next few times, she just seemed uneasy, and ran her hands through her sandy, stormy hair to show she was displeased. Then, one day, I was the one who got detention.

She wondered out loud why I had turned into such a stool pigeon. I said I wasn't a bird, even if I was sitting on a stool. When she got upset, the teacher thought I was a birdbrain, so I thought the storm wasn't only in her hair, but inside her head, too. Then she said not to do her any more favors, that that kind of favor wasn't nice. She didn't want to have eyes in the back of her head, and she had every right not to. And then she took the bump out of her sleeve and blew her nose in it, so I asked if it was always the same tissue. Her only answer was to squeeze it very tightly in her hand and scream at me to get out. In the hall I wondered why she'd made such an issue of a tissue, and decided that you really couldn't get anything out of that teacher but mucus.

When I told my mother the story about eyes in the back of the teacher's head, she thought it was my imagination and crowed, "Informer, what a lovely occupation! It's perfectly perfect, my boy! Thanks to you, all will be right with the world." With all the lying backward and forward, sometimes I really didn't know which way I was supposed to go.

After writing, we had to learn how to read the time on a clock with hands on its face. That was a real calamity, because even though I already knew how to read the time on my father's watch with numbers that glowed in the dark, I just couldn't read it on the clock whose hands didn't glow at all. Something to do with the light, I figured. Not being able to read the time was bad enough, but not being able to read it in front of the whole class was even worse. For weeks on end, there were clocks on all the chemical-smelling ditto sheets we got. And that whole time, boats were sailing by, as the teacher pointed out. "If you don't learn to tell time soon, you'll miss every last boat!" she said, giving the other children a laugh at my expense.

She asked my mother to come in again to talk about my transportation problems and completely forgot to mention that I was turning into a bird. My mother, who had clock issues herself, got very angry and scolded her, "My son already knows how to read the time on his father's watch, and that's plenty good enough nowadays! Did farmers keep teaching their sons how to plow with horses after tractors were invented? I don't think so!"

It was a perfectly sensible remark, but the teacher never relented. Instead, she looked at my mom like she was demented, and yelled that our whole family was one big bowl of nuts. She'd never seen anything like it, she lamented, then added that from then on, she would leave me alone and not worry about me anymore. Then she showed Mom the door.

"At noon that same day, mere moments after the bell, with the ditto-paper clock ticking out its awful smell, staring outside while daydreaming, our stunned son took comfort in watching the playground morph into a moat with a wake left by that other life, sailing away in a boat."

After they had taken me out of school, my parents would often say that they had offered me early retirement. "You must be the youngest retiree in the world!" my father would say, chortling in that childlike way that grown-ups—or at least my parents—sometimes have.

They seemed thrilled to have me by their side all day long, and I didn't have to worry about missing all those boats anymore. I had no regrets whatsoever about leaving my class or my teacher with her turbulent hair and faux cancer of the sleeve.

My parents had no shortage of ideas for how to educate me. For math lessons, they draped me in bracelets, necklaces and rings, and had me count them for addition. Then they'd strip me down to my long johns for subtraction. They called that my "arithme-tease," and it left us doubled over with laughter. For more complicated math, Dad would give me an "immersion course," as he put it. He'd fill the bathtub, with me in it, and scoop out pints, quarts and gallons, asking me a multitude of technical questions. Whenever I got the answer wrong, he would pour a quart of water over my head. My math lessons were more like pool parties, I have to admit.

The two of them composed an entire repertory of songs to teach me conjugation, with hand gestures for personal pronouns. I learned those lessons by heart, and was perfectly happy to dance to the past-tense song all day long. At night,

I read them stories that I had written myself, or summaries of stories that had already been written by the classics.

The best thing about my early retirement was that we could go to Spain without having to wait for everyone else. Sometimes the need to go came over us like having to pee, although it did take a little longer to deal with. In the morning, Dad would say, "Pauline, let's get packing. I want to have cocktails by the lake tonight!" So we'd toss tons of things into our suitcases. There'd be stuff flying all over the place. Dad would shout at the top of his voice, "Jill, where are my espadrilles?"

Mom would answer, "In the garbage, George! That's where they look best!" Or she would toss out, "George, don't forget your foolishness, we always need it!"

And my father would shoot back, "Don't worry, Connie, I always keep a copy on me!" We always forgot all sorts of things, but then we were usually knocking ourselves out to get to Spain in a New York minute.

Down there, everything was different, but the mountain was in a hurry, too. With its wintry, snow-capped peak, the autumnal reds and browns of the sunbaked earth and rocks just below it, the juicy spring colors of the terraced

orchards, and the summery heat and smells reverberat-
ing off the lake in the valley, Dad used to say that with a
mountain like that, you could dash through a year in less
than a day.

Since we went whenever we felt like it, we usually felt
like arriving when the almond trees were in bloom, and
leaving after the orange blossoms had fallen. In between,
we'd paddle around the lake, tan grease-free without
fouling our towels, have huge barbecues and invite lots of
people over for drinks. In the morning, I'd fish the chunks
of fruit out of the glasses and make myself a fruit salad so
big that the bowl would be overflowing. The guests would
be amazed that it was always fiesta time, and Dad would
say good, that was how life should be.

When Parliament was on vacation, the Creep would
come to visit. He said that senators were like children,
they needed to get their rest. To show that he was work-
less, he'd wear a straw hat and go shirtless all day long,
which was pretty impressive, considering how plump and
hairy his stomach was. He'd spend the whole day on the
terrace enjoying the view, eating, and drinking fruit. In the
evening, he'd call for his girlfriend, and you could hear
"Caipiroska-aa-aaaa-aa!" echoing down the valley.

He used to say that he would feel that he had succeeded in life when he could balance a place setting on his stomach. So he ate and drank all the time, to give himself every chance for success.

When he first got to Spain, the sun would turn him redder than usual. Papa said that it was "beyond reason," which I figured was the name of a very deep, powerful red, hard to get past on a color chart. As the vacation wore on, the Senator would go totally brown. When he was snoozing, I loved to watch his hairy belly sweat. There were always minuscule rivers running through the hair and pooling in his belly button.

The Creep and I would play "Russian Droolette," a game he had invented just for me. We would sit facing each other and open our mouths as wide as we could. The idea was to toss anchovy-stuffed olives or salted almonds at each other. Our faces were the targets, and our mouths, the bulls'-eyes. You had to aim really carefully, because the anchovies stung our eyes (though not the bulls'), and so did the salt from the almonds. Since the games lasted a long time, we always wound up drooling all over ourselves.

When Dad was working on a book, the Creep would come hiking in the mountains with Mom and me. It would always start out the same way, with him way ahead of us, saying that hiking brought back memories of his time in the army. But we'd catch up with him as his memories started wandering away, and we'd start to pull ahead when he'd used up his memories and was dripping with sweat. So we'd leave him sitting on a rock and go eat wild asparagus and prickly pears, and pick thyme and rosemary and pine nuts. By the time we found him on our way back down, he would have dried off completely.

He did take things seriously occasionally, like when he would give me advice for my future. I was really struck by one thing that he'd said was, "just horse sense," to emphasize how logical and important it was: "My boy, if you don't want to get double-crossed, there are two categories of people to avoid at all costs: vegetarians and professional cyclists. The first, because anyone who refuses to eat a rib steak must have been a cannibal in another life. And the second, because a man who goes out with a suppository on his head and shoves his nuts into fluorescent tights to climb mountains on a bicycle can't be all there. So if you ever meet a vegetarian cyclist, here's a piece of advice, little man: give him a good shove to save time, then run far away, as fast as you can!" I thanked him for his wise counsel, declaring gratefully, "The most dangerous enemies are the ones you least suspect!" For all I knew, he had just saved my life, and even though I didn't see how horse sense could teach you anything about cyclists, I decided to keep it in mind.

For Mom's birthday, my father and the Creep would row the boat out early in the morning to set fireworks up in the middle of the lake, while Mom and I would go to the market to buy bottles, fruit, ham, paella, chorizo, round bracelets of squid, cake and ice cream, and I don't know how many more bottles. When we got back, Mom would ask me to use my powers to entertain her with stories while she looked for the perfect outfit, which always took hours. She would try clothes on; ask for my opinion, which was always approving; then ask for the mirror's. The mirror always got the last word, because, she said, "your outlook is moving, but the mirror's is more objective. It judges truthfully, if cruelly, and never gets affected by the affective."

Then she'd change again, swan around to see how the clothes moved, dance in her lingerie, decide it was perfectly perfect, but perhaps not right for today, and start over yet again, putting the same clothes on, but differently. Staccato sounds of setup—laughter, shouting and some shrieks—would rise from the lake.

"Not like that, Cre-eee-eee-eep," Dad's voice would echo.

"We're sin-n-n-k-k-k-ing!" the Creep would respond.

"Sit STIIIILLLLLL!!!!" my father would beg him.

"Cheeeeers!" they would chime in chorus.

As if by magic, Mom would find the right outfit just minutes before the guests arrived. Every time, it was totally amazing. Then she'd paint her lips, brush her long eyelashes on and be ready to welcome people with such natural grace that you'd think she'd rolled out of bed like that. Her perfect presentation was a lie, too, but what a splendid lie it was.

Waiting for night to fall over the terrace all draped in white, people drank and complimented each other's tans, their outfits and their wives, and congratulated themselves for the splendid weather, even though they didn't have anything to do with it. Wearing a custom-made necklace of small change, Mademoiselle Superfluous strolled haughtily amongst the guests, never hesitating to peck at bits of grilled squid, splattering nearby pants legs with olive oil.

Then, once the last wedge of the sun had disappeared into the valley below, "Bojangles" would ring out, floating into the atmosphere on Nina Simone's warm, sweet voice and the echo of her piano. It was so beautiful that everyone stopped talking to watch Mom cry soundlessly. With one hand, I wiped away her tears, and with the other, I held hers. I usually saw the first fireworks in her eyes: the colorful bouquets scattering like confetti in the sky, moving in the opposite direction in their reflection in the lake. Those double fireworks would leave everyone dumbstruck and gaping, then little by little, you would start to hear clapping. As faint as water lapping the shore at first, it would grow louder and louder, blending in with the sounds from the bursts of gunpowder. It would rumble and growl, snap, crackle and pop, fade out and then roar up again even louder. After the grand finale, as the fiery spangles from the loudest, biggest and highest blast had started drifting gently down toward the starry blanket of the lake, Mom would whisper wistfully in my ear, "He jumped so high, he jumped so high, then he'd lightly touch down."

And then we'd dance.

4.

"Don't tell me you're leaving for work again! You're going to work yourself into an early grave, my dear man. What day can it be?" she groaned, abandoning her pillow to cling to me.

"It's Saturday, Desirée. Today is Saturday, and my garages are open on Saturdays, so I'm working today, as I do almost every day," I answered, as I did every morning, happy to let myself be clung to by her warm and cuddly body.

"Oh, it's true, you still work on Saturdays, don't you, but please tell me this laborious nonsense isn't going to go on much longer."

"I'm afraid it might go on for quite a while. You may not be aware of it, but that is how most of the world lives," I replied, trying to coax her grouchy face back into a smile.

"Well then, tell me why our young downstairs neighbor never has to go to work on Saturdays?" she asked defiantly, rolling on top of me to plunge her inquiring eyes deep into mine.

"Because he's a schoolboy, my dear lady, and children don't have school on Saturdays."

"What a bother! I should have married a child rather than my own grandfather. My life wouldn't have been so bleak, at least not on Saturdays," she said mournfully, ignoring my proffered cheek.

"I suppose so, but it's a very bad thing to do. And it's neither legal nor moral."

"Perhaps not, but at least children can enjoy themselves on Saturdays, while I get bored waiting for you. I never know what to do! I feel left on a shelf here all day by myself. So why doesn't the man on the first floor ever work either? I see him taking out his garbage every day at four when I'm on my way to the grocery store. His eyes are puffy and his hair's all choppy, and his clothes are always very sloppy. Don't try to tell me that he's still in school or I'll know you're taking me for a fool!"

"No, for the man on the first floor, it's a different story. He's lost his job, and I bet he'd be thrilled to have to work on Saturdays, the poor slob."

"Wouldn't you know it? I gave my hand to the only fellow around who works on Saturdays," she mumbled, looking peeved and aggrieved, one hand over her eyes, as if to spare herself the sight of an unbearable reality.

"If you're looking for something to keep you busy, I've got an idea . . ."

"Oh, you and your sordid ideas. You want me to get a job, but no way! I've already told you, I tried it once, on a Thursday."

"I remember it very well, my belle. You worked for a florist for a few hours, but they fired you, because you refused to take money for the flowers."

"Well, I should certainly hope not! What is the world coming to? You can't sell flowers, flowers are free! You just bend over and pick them. Flowers are life, and as far as I am aware, you can't sell life! And besides, they didn't fire me, I left of my own accord. I didn't want to have anything to do with their scam, which I abhorred. While the others were on their lunch break, I decided to take the biggest bouquet I could make. I had so much fun, it was a scream, and then I left with the most beautiful bouquet anyone has ever seen."

"I compliment you on managing to be a stickler for principles while having sticky fingers. Everybody knows Mr. Robin Hood, but I married Miss Robbin' Flowers! But that's not actually what I was thinking of, my love. You refuse to seek gainful employment, as you'd much rather, let's say, focus on your own enjoyment. That much I gather, but since you've got nothing else to do, surely you wouldn't refuse to help our

neighbor, would you? Our address book is overflowing with VIPs, someone's bound to be able to help him with ease. And that way, perhaps I won't be the only fellow here who has to work on Saturday."

"What a wonderful notion! I'm going to swing right into motion, and help our neighbor get a promotion! We'll organize a great job-hunt lunch, with a big bunch of your VIP pals and their gals. I'm sure we'll arrange a transaction to everybody's satisfaction. But first, I'm going to take him shopping for decent clothes and shoes, because everyone knows, if you want a fresh start, you've got to look the part!" Cheering with exuberance, she turned the bed into a trampoline for an airborne dance. Well, that was the best-case scenario, anyway.

Ever since that firecracker day we met, she had pretended to be charmingly ignorant of the way the world worked. Or at least, I pretended to believe she was pretending, because it came to her so naturally. After the incident at the pool, we fled the hotel, leaving behind our prank, the outraged entrepreneurs, and that poor, nasty woman who nearly sank. With the top down, we rode out of town and off into the sunset, singing splish-splash and glug-glug-glug, and laughing like crazy as we drove through the night.

"Speed up, don't be lazy, or your lies are going to catch up

with us, and that woman's going to make a fuss!" she shouted, standing up. "But we won't mind her," she added, her shawl fluttering behind her.

"I can't go any faster, the speedometer is as high as it can go, and the gas gauge as low. Besides, at the rate we're going, our truancy is going to crash into your lunacy any minute now anyhow!"

In a village called Paradou, in the hills of Provence, the automobile started trembling miserably, as if begging for mercy, then it stalled for good in front of a chapel with doors of worn red wood, topped with a rusty iron pineapple.

"Let's get married right away, lest we forget we've met!" said my soon-to-be-blushing bride, leaping over the door with clumsy pride. We got married then and there, with no priest and no witnesses, but thousands of prayers, and vows of our own invention. In front of the altar, we sang and clapped like the faithful at a gospel church. I knew I'd never leave her in the lurch. Stepping outside again, we heard a tune wafting from the car radio, a lovely song by Nina Simone, a song that still reverberates through our lives at all hours of the day and night.

The extravagant behavior of my new wife soon took over my life, nestling in every corner, occupying every minute, de-

vouring every instant. I had welcomed her folly with open arms, then closed them to hug it close and soak it in, but I was afraid that such sweet madness couldn't go on happily ever after. For her, real life didn't exist. I had married a female Don Quixote who seemed permanently high on peyote. Every morning, her eyes still swollen with sleep, onto her exhausted nag she'd leap, spurring it on with frantic antics as she galloped up the hill to tilt at the next windmill.

My Sweet Charity had brought great clarity to my life by turning it into constant chaos. Her path was clear, she was headed every which way at once, and I had no objections to her moving in a thousand directions. My role was to dance attendance on all that resplendence, to enable her to revel with the devil in her insanity rather than get bogged down at the level of mundane reality.

When we saw a wounded crane by the side of a path in Africa one day, she wanted to keep it and tend it until its leg was mended. So we extended our stay by nearly two weeks, and when the bird was better, despite its shrieks, she insisted that the crane should fly back to Paris in the plane with us. But my darling Starling couldn't understand that we needed to cover mountains of certificates with stamps in order to bring an exotic bird back to France.

"This fowl nonsense makes no sense! Don't tell me that

every time my crane flies over a border she has to deal with all this paperwork and red-taper work!" she railed and wailed as she flailed around, pounding on the vet's desk, making a mess.

Another time, we had invited a scientist to dinner. The poor man, who meant no harm, was explaining that the expression "a castle in the air" or "a castle in Spain" meant something that wasn't really there. Her green eyes began to sparkle with defiance. "So much for science! Say what you may, but a year from today, we'll be drinking champagne in our castle in Spain! The castle will be in the air, I swear, but the drinks will be on you, so you'd better beware!"

To win that bet, we had to fly to the Mediterranean Costas every weekend for months before we managed to find a huge house topped with a crenellated turret that seemed to float above the clouds in a mist-shrouded valley. The people in the village below, meaning well, had nicknamed it "El Castel."

Living like that required complete devotion, so when I finally offered her the child she had been demanding of me every morning, I was struck by the notion that one day, without warning, I would have to give up my garages, liquidate everything and devote myself to my charges. I knew her madness could go off the rails someday. I couldn't be sure, but with a child, it was my duty to be ready anyway. With a niño *in the mix, there could be so much more to fix. For all I knew, the countdown might already have started. And it was on the strength of that "might" that we danced and threw parties day and night.*

5.

$\mathcal{I}$t was shortly after one of her birthdays that Mom's metamorphosis began. *"It was barely visible to the naked eye, but there was a change in the mood, in her personal weather. We didn't really see anything, we just felt it. Little nothings, a change of tempo in the way she moved and grooved, batted her eyelashes, clapped her hands. At first, to tell you the whole truth, we didn't see it, we only sensed it. We assumed that her originality had kept rising, that she had reached the next level. Then she began to get upset more frequently, for longer periods, but nothing alarming. She was still charming, still danced like before, or perhaps even more, with even greater abandon and enthusiasm, but nothing worrisome. She was drinking a bit more, cocktails and such, sometimes before she got out of bed in the morning, but the time of day and the amount didn't really change much, didn't affect the way we lived. We kept on as we had always done, with our parties, our castle and our life of fun."* That's what my father wrote about what happened.

It was the doorbell that revealed my mother's new nature. Or rather the person who rang it. With his sunken cheeks, that peculiar complexion that only an office job can supply, and a sense of duty that leaked onto his gabardine, the tax assessor explained to my parents that they had forgotten to pay their income taxes for a very long time—so long, in fact, that he had a big file under his arm, because his memory alone wouldn't suffice. My father, trying to be cheerful, didn't give him an earful. With a smile stuck on his face, despite being a tad hungover, he filled his pipe and went to get his checkbook off the table in the hall, the one the painting of the Prussian hung over. But my father's face and pipe both fell when the tax man stated the amount of taxes due, plus the little something for the late fees, too. Those alone were humongous, so the amount of taxes themselves could have bowled you over. Actually, they wound up bowling the tax man over instead: Mom started shoving him away so frantically that he fell. Dad tried to calm her down and to help him up, boastfully offering his humblest apologies. The tax man didn't let Dad help him up, although he did get carried away, stuttering, "You have to pay now! It's good for everyone to, to, to p-p-pay your t-t-taxes! You're happy enough to have paved streets to walk on! You are un-un-un-scru-pu-pu-lous!"

"You villainous varlet! How dare you insult us on top of everything!" Mom replied, screaming with unprecedented ferocity. "We don't walk the streets! I'm not that kind of harlot! Hotel rooms, perhaps, but streetwalking? Never! And if paying taxes is so great, then go ahead, enjoy yourself, pay ours!" As Dad tried to relight his pipe, keeping a perplexed eye on Mom, she grabbed the umbrella by the door, opened it, and used it to chase the tax assessor out of our apartment.

Backing out onto the landing, the tax man shouted hoarsely, "That's going to cost you a pretty penny, too. You're going to have to cough up every last cent. I'm going to turn your lives into a descent into tax hell!"

My mother, using the umbrella like a shield, tried to send the swordsman of the taxocalypse hurtling down the stairs, while he clung to the banister, grunting valiantly. He would fall, haul himself up again, slip and catch himself. Mom really put his sense of duty to the test, giving him no respite or rest. For an instant, I even caught his long career flashing before his stubborn red eyes. By the time Dad managed to stop her by hugging her tight, she had gotten the taxes down several brackets, or rather flights. After two threatening calls on the interphone, the tax man went to get money to pave the streets from other people. The three of us had a good laugh about the whole thing, until Dad asked, "Really, Hortense, what came over you? Or what got into you? We're going to be in serious trouble now."

"We're in serious trouble already, my poor George! That's right, you're poor now, George. We're all poor! And that's so commonplace, so trivial, so sad. We're going to have to sell the apartment, and you're asking what got into me? It's not what got *into* me but what they'll be getting *out* of us: everything, George, everything! We won't have even one pretty penny . . . ," she replied. Then she suddenly spun around, looking panic-stricken, as if she wanted to make sure the apartment was still there.

"But, Hortense, we haven't lost everything, we'll find a solution. Perhaps the Senator can provide absolution. And in the future, we'll open the mail, though I fear it might be to no avail," my father sighed, glancing at the mountain of paper with more than a touch of administrative regret.

"Not *Hortense*! Not today! They've even taken my real name away; I don't even have a name anymore," she said, sobbing like a fountain, collapsing mournfully onto the mail mountain.

"Selling the apartment will fetch plenty more than our debt, so you needn't fret. We still have our castle in the air, which is not exactly a hovel, you know. And I could always get another job."

"Oh, no, over my dead body! As long as I'm alive, you'll never work again! Do you hear me? Never!" she screamed hysterically, tossing the letters in the air, like a baby splashing the bathwater in despair. "Your place is with the two of us! I can't spend my days waiting for you. I can't live without you! Not even for one single second, but certainly not for a whole day! In fact, I wonder how other people manage it," she whispered, her voice breaking into sobs, gliding from rage to hopelessness in just a few words.

That night in my room, contemplating the two beds I would have to leave behind, I wondered why the Senator hadn't warned me about tax assessors. What if ours had been a vegetarian cyclist, too? I couldn't even bear to think about it. We may have been lucky after all, I realized with a shiver of fright, before transpiercing Claude François with precision, but without delight.

Between the appeals board and the Creep pulling strings, our lives weren't completely upended in a day. The procedures took time, so we didn't have to move out right away. After her bout of toxic-shock syndrome, my mother's behavior went back to how it had been. Or, almost, anyway. Sometimes, during dinner parties, she would get this odd grin, then start laughing so hard she couldn't stop, going on and on until she had slid under the table, and was banging her hands on the parquet floor.

Depending on the dinner guests, and the subjects being addressed, either everyone's laughter would mingle with hers, or else the table would go silent, the guests not speaking or smiling or comprehending her laughter unending. When that happened, Dad would help her up, whispering sweet, soothing nothings in her ear and wiping the wild streams of makeup from her cheeks. He would lead her to their bedroom and stay as long as necessary. Sometimes it took so long that the guests left, tiptoeing out to avoid disturbing them. For laughing fits, they were strangely sad.

The problem with Mom's new state of mind, as Dad put it, was that you never knew where you were standing, let alone dancing. And when it came to dancing, you could take his word for it, because he was an expert. Sometimes she wouldn't have a single fit—of either laughter, anger or despair—for weeks on end, long enough for us to forget about her spells of confusion and bad manners. During those periods, she seemed more adorable than ever, and even more lovable than before, which wasn't easily feasible, though she pulled it off breezily.

The problem with Mom's new state of mind was that it

had no schedule, no set time; it didn't make appointments. It just showed up without warning, the cad. It would patiently wait for us to forget all about it and go back to our old lives, and then it would pop up unannounced, morning, noon or night: during dinner, after a shower, when we were out for a stroll. And when that happened, we never knew what to do or how to do it, even though, after a while, we should have gotten used to it.

There are first-aid manuals that tell you how to act in case of an accident, how to save people's lives, but there were none for this sort of thing. You never get used to it. So with each and every new alarm, Dad and I would stare at each other, completely disarmed. For the first few seconds, anyway. Afterward, we'd remember. Then we'd look around to see where the relapse could be coming from. But it wasn't coming *from* anywhere, it was just there, and that was exactly the problem.

We had our lot of sad laughter, too. One evening, when a dinner guest kept saying "I'll bet my bloomers" every time he declared anything, we watched Mom stand, lift her skirt up, pull down her panties trimmed with lace, then silently take them off and throw them in the gambler's face. Those panties sailed over the table, landing smack on his nose. So it goes. After a shocked silence, a lady blurted out, "She's lost her mind!"

To which my mother replied, having downed her glass in one gulp, "No, ma'am, at worst, I've lost my panties."

The Creep, that wonderful fellow, saved the day. He bellowed and guffawed, and the chilly atmosphere soon thawed, turning the nascent drama into a saucy story of flying lingerie. If the Creep hadn't laughed, no one else would have either though. Like the other guests, Dad had laughed until he cried, but with his face in his hands.

One morning at my breakfast time, when my parents hadn't gone to bed yet and a few dancers were still going at it in the living room, making strange noises, when the Creep was sleeping on the kitchen table, with his nose on his cigar and his cigar crushed into an ashtray, and Mademoiselle Superfluous was doing her dormitory rounds, waking the soiree's stragglers, I saw my mother step out of the bathroom perched on stiletto heels, stark naked except for the smoke from her cigarette that fleetingly garbed her face. Looking for her keys on the table in the front hall, she informed my father in a perfectly natural tone of voice that she was off to get oysters and cold muscadet for their guests.

"Cover up, Marigold, or you're going to catch your death of cold," he said with a concerned smile.

"You're absolutely right, George, what would I do without you! I love you, monsieur, did you know that?" she answered as she grabbed a fur hat from the rack.

Then she disappeared, just a beat ahead of the startling sound of the door slamming. My father and I watched her from the balcony, striding regally, all-conquering chin up, ignoring the strange looks, taming the sidewalks, flicking away her cigarette, wiping her dancing shoes on the doormat before stepping inside the fish shop. My father answered her, belatedly, whispering with veiled eyes, "Yes, I do know you love me, Dove, but what am I supposed to do with all that crazy love? What *am* I supposed to do with all that crazy love?"

Then Mom stepped out of the shop, smiling toward us as though she had heard him, with a tray of oysters perched on one arm, and two bottles squashing her breasts under the other. "She's a miracle," he sighed. "I couldn't live without her. It's inconceivable. That craziness belongs to me, too."

Sometimes she would throw herself into crackpot schemes with surprising enthusiasm. Then the enthusiasm would vanish, and the schemes as well; only the surprises stuck around. When she started writing her novel, she ordered reams of paper and boxes of pencils for writing, plus an encyclopedia, a big desk and a desk lamp. She moved the desk from one window to another, for inspiration, then pushed it against a wall, for concentration. But once she sat down, when neither concentration nor inspiration could be found, she'd get mad, toss the paper in the air, break the pencils meant for writing, pound her fists on the desk and turn out the lighting. Her novel was over without a single phrase having been scribbled on that ton of paper.

Later, she decided to paint the apartment to increase its value. She shopped—for paint, brushes, rollers, toxic solvents, ladders, masking tape and rolls of plastic to protect the furniture, the parquet and the baseboards—until she dropped. Then, after draping the whole apartment in plastic and dabbing every imaginable shade of paint onto the walls, she gave the whole project up, saying she didn't give a toss. All was lost, no matter what, and with or without paint, selling the place was our lot. For weeks, our apartment looked exactly like a huge walk-in freezer filled with food packaged compactly.

Dad couldn't bring himself to tease her; there was no point in trying to reason with her either. She did it all so matter-of-factly, not seeing what was the matter, that he gave up on all of his dreams. He watched his wife vanish down the rabbit hole, as mad as a hatter, along with her incongruous schemes. The real problem was that she was losing her mind and didn't know where to find it. My father's voice wasn't enough to soothe her anymore, it seemed.

One boringly ordinary afternoon, our lives went up in smoke. Thick, coal-black, chemical smoke. While my father and I were out shopping—for fine wine, bread and cheese, dish detergent and fresh peas—he decided we absolutely had to go to Mom's favorite florist. "Lily adores his compositions; he's far away, but her smile will make it worth the delay!" The delay was indeed a long one, what with the traffic, the numerous and punctilious clients, our meticulous search for a composition that was perfectly harmonious, more traffic, the hunt for a parking place, and then, in our street, a huge cloud. We were out of luck: in front of our building was a fire truck. From our living-room windows, thick dark smoke poured, while firemen fought a fire that roared, and flames licked crazily at our window frames. To reach the truck and the sirens' din, we had to shove our way in through a huge mass of gawkers who didn't want to let us through, despite our screams and hullabaloo. "Calm down, kid, stop pushing!" said a man who was blocking our way. "Besides, you're too late, there's nothing left to see anyway!" Dad had to punch him in the eye before he'd let us get by.

"Flowers! Aren't you two just too sweet!" Mom exclaimed, from under a shiny golden sheet. She was lying on the stretcher the firefighters had used to fetch her from the flaming inferno. She was safe, but there were no words to express our distress. Her face was streaked black and gray from the ash flurries, but she smiled as though she had no worries, even as our world crumbled around her. It nearly broke my heart when she said with good cheer, "Everything's settled, my dears. I burned all our souvenirs, at least that's one thing they won't commandeer! Oh la la, it was hot in there, but everything's fine now, except for my hair!" Then she tried to pat it back into place, as a fetching smile lit up her face.

There were spitballs of burnt plastic stuck to her bare shoulders. "It's all over, it's all over," my father mumbled between sighs. At a loss for words, he just patted her forehead, querying her with his eyes. No questions asked, no names given. Taking a breather from words, I settled for nibbling gently at her pitch-black hands, softening their harsh complexion with my noiseless affection.

The fire chief explained that she had moved the mountain of mail into the living room, then piled all the photos in the house on top of it; she'd set fire to it all, and with the plastic sheets lining the walls, our living room had turned into a gigantic cauldron. They had found her crouching calmly in a corner of the front hall, holding a turntable and a large, panic-stricken bird. She had minor burns from the paper blaze, but nothing serious. Only the living room was affected; the rest of our apartment and the building had been spared. In a nutshell, the fire chief said, we had fared pretty well, and everything was almost all right. Although that remained to be seen.

Nobody seemed to be able to show us the proof that everything was almost all right. Certainly not the police officers who interrogated Mom for a long time, stunned by her dancer's regal poise and her answers' surreal noise. "All I did was to destroy what I didn't want to lose! Without all those stupid sheets of plastic, none of this would have happened!" "No, I don't have anything against the neighbors. If I had wanted to burn them out, I would have set fire to their apartment, not my own!" "You want to know how I feel? Frankly, what's the big deal? So much fuss, over a few bits of burnt paper that belonged to us!" Watching her answering their questions so cheerfully and calmly, Dad grabbed my hand so I wouldn't let go of him.

His eyes seemed dim. When they hosed our place down to put out the blaze, the firemen extinguished the light I'd always known in Dad's gaze. He was becoming more and more like the Prussian cavalier in the painting: his face was young but cracked, and his clothes had obviously seen better days. Like them, he seemed to come from another era, his own having just come crashing to an end. You could look at him, but you couldn't ask him anything.

The clinic wasn't able to show us the proof that everything was almost all right either. Only Mom thought everything was marvelous. "Why are we going to such a grim place? We could be dancing, it would be so much more entrancing than this! They sealed off the living room, but we can still dance in the dining room! Let's play 'Bojangles'! The record escaped unscathed! It's so nice out today, isn't there anywhere else we could play?" she chattered away lightheartedly. When we didn't reply, she got a sad look in her eye. "You're really no fun, my husband and son," she groused, before setting foot inside that bleak house.

When we first entered that place, and she saw the doctor's concerned face, she teased him, looking pleased with herself. "My poor man, what's wrong, why the face so long? If you have some time to kill, you should see a doctor for a pill! I suppose that being with the mentally ill all day long, you wind up taking some of it on, but you really don't seem well. Even your white coat looks like hell!" Her quips elicited a wan smile from my dad, but absolutely not from the doctor, who asked with a sideways glance to be left alone with her. The discussion lasted three hours, and my father never stopped smoking as we paced back and forth in front of the depressing building.

"You'll see, this nightmare's going to be over soon," he kept saying over and over. "Everything's going to be okay. She'll get better, and when she returns, we'll fête her. She's as pretty and witty as ever, no one that funny could be completely done for!" He said it so often that he wound up convincing me, and himself, too. So when the doctor asked to speak to him alone, he gave me a wink. A wink that meant this nightmare was going to be over soon.

The doctor must not have agreed. When my father came back, the sight of his face was enough. In the blink of an eye, I knew that the wink had been an unwitting lie. "They're going to keep your mother under observation for a bit, 'til they can get to the bottom of it. When she gets out, she'll be as fresh as a daisy. It's better that way. In the meantime, we'll come to see her every day. This will all be over soon, so we mustn't be lazy. We'll get to work right away, fixing things up for her homecoming day. You pick the color for the paint, perhaps something quaint? We'll have a great time, don't worry—everything's going to be hunky-dory!" he said with his mouth. But his sad eyes told a different story. My father never said anything untoward, but for my sake, he too was capable of lying backward and forward.

6.

The doctors explained that we had to protect her from herself in order to protect everyone else. Dad said that only doctors could come up with such a stupid thing to say. Mom was ensconced on the third floor of the clinic, with the people whose brains had moved out. Actually, for most of them, the move was still ongoing. Their minds were leaving little by little, so they chomped on pills as they waited patiently for everything to be taken away. In the hallway, there were lots of people who looked full and whole on the outside, but they were actually pretty much empty on the inside. The third floor was a gigantic antechamber to the fourth, where the mentally decapitated were. Patients on the fourth floor were a lot more fun. For them, the moving van had come and gone. The pills had cleared everything out, leaving nothing but madness and wind. When Dad wanted to be alone with Mom, for a slow dance with feeling, or to do things I was too young to understand, I liked to go for a stroll upstairs.

Upstairs, there was Sven, my new Dutch friend, who spoke dozens of languages, often in the same sentences. Sven had wild hair and a nice face, with a weird tooth that stuck out in front and made him spray spittle everywhere. In his life before, Sven used to be an engineer, so he jotted tons of statistics down in his notebook. He could come across a little gruff, but he knew all sorts of important stuff. Like polo scores, for instance. You could ask him about any game, he'd flip though his notebook with insistence, and eventually, voilà! He'd find the score, and the winning team's name, scribbled on some crumpled page. It was amazing.

You could tell Sven had been to college, he was a regular fount of knowledge. The moving van had missed one room in his head that was still full to bursting. He was fascinated by the lives of the popes, too. He could tell you their nationality and date of birth, the length of their reign and even their girth. But what Sven liked most of all was pop music in French. He always had his Walkman attached to his belt and headphones around his neck. He was a regular jukebox, wandering around in his slippers and socks.

He had a nice loud voice, and he put his heart and soul into it, which made his mouth water with delight. I would step back a bit when he sang, because I hated to get spittle on my face. Once Sven sang a Claude François song about a hammer in French, and I finally understood why Dad had turned Claude into a dartboard. If I had a hammer, I would have smashed Sven's Walkman so he would stop singing that awful tune. But otherwise, I liked his songs, and I could listen to him sing all afternoon. I loved when he'd flap his arms like wings and sing at the same time. It really made you want to fly away with him. Sven alone was happier than all the doctors and nurses put together.

There was Air Bubble, too. I made that name up for her, because she never answered when I asked her her name. Everybody should have a name, I thought, or at least a nickname. It's better if you want to introduce them to someone. So I came up with one. With Air Bubble, it was clear: the meds had moved everything out, not a single box had been left behind. She was mentally decapitated full-time. She always had a sheet of movers' bubble wrap in her hands, and she'd spend the whole day bursting the bubbles, staring at the ceiling and nibbling pills.

She took other medications through her veins because

she didn't have much of an appetite. Her arm could swallow gallons without getting an ounce fatter, and even if she had, it didn't really matter. A nurse told me that before she had moved out, Air Bubble had done some really nasty things, so the tablets kept her demons from refurnishing her brain. She popped bubbles because her head was full of air. That way, she was always in her element. When I'd had enough of Sven's French songs, I'd go stare at the ceiling with Air Bubble. Listening to the little crackling sounds of the bubble wrap was very peaceful. Sometimes Air Bubble let her air escape all over the place, and then you had to run, because there was no medicine that could do anything about that.

Air Bubble got a lot of visits from Yogurt, a weird guy who thought he was the president. His nickname wasn't my idea, it was the staff's. They called him that because his body overflowed from his clothes, and his skin was all pale and mushy. It really looked like he was going to ooze away on the spot. His brain had moved out, but the pills had moved a brand-spanking-new one in. Yogurt had these strange warts on his face, and he always had cookie crumbs around his lips. It was really off-putting. To hide how ugly he was, he dyed and shellacked his hair, standing it up in the back. He must have thought it was chic to have a crow wing sticking out like a beak. He spent so much time with Air Bubble that everybody at the clinic figured he must have had a crush on her. He would spend hours watching her burble and crush bubbles, while he told her what it was like to be president. All his sentences began with *me, me, me,* which was really exhausting after a while.

In the hallways, he would glad-hand everybody he saw with a seriously funny look on his face, because he wanted their votes. Every Friday night he'd hold a political rally, then he'd organize an election with a cardboard ballot box. Sven would count the ballots and write down the tally in his notebook, then he would sing the results until Yogurt stood up on a chair to give his acceptance speech. He was a bit of a ham, but those elections made him as happy as a clam. Dad said he was a fool, with all the charisma of a kitchen stool, but everybody liked him anyway. He may have made a perfectly ridiculous president, but he was a perfectly nice patient.

At first, Mom was bored stiff on the third floor. She said that if she had to be sent to the funny farm, she might as well be kicked upstairs to the fourth floor. She thought her third-floor neighbors were depressing, and moaned

that the meds were no blessing. Her moods were unpre-
dictable. She might be charming when we arrived, but go
into hysterics when we were leaving. Or the other way
around, which made it hard to stay. You had to be patient
until the patient calmed down, and that could take awhile.
Dad would keep the same smile plastered on his face the
whole time. I thought it was strong and comforting, but on
her bad days, my mother thought it was annoyingly cloy-
ing. It wasn't an easy time for any of us.

Fortunately, she had kept her sense of humor. She would
do imitations of her neighbors for us: twisting up her face,
slurring her words when she talked and dragging her feet as
she walked. One afternoon, we got there to find her deep
in conversation with a little bald guy who was wringing his
hands and staring at his feet. He was strange looking: his
face was all wrinkly, but his scalp was perfectly smooth.
"Perfect timing, George, let me introduce you to my lover.
You wouldn't think so to look at him, but he can be quite
the stud when he wants to be!" she declared, stroking his
scalp as he nodded his head and giggled. Dad stepped in
to shake Baldy's hand. "Thank you, my friend," he said.
"Let's make a deal: you take care of her when she's screaming, and I'll take over when she's smiling. You'll come out

ahead, because she spends a lot more time screaming than smiling!" Mom burst out laughing, Dad and I did, too, and Baldy followed our lead and laughed even harder.

"Now get out of here, you big screwball you, and come back in an hour or two. Who knows, maybe I'll feel like screaming at you!" she said to Baldy, who was giggling on his way out the door.

Another time, she greeted us with her head drooping, her arms hanging over the sides of her chair and drool oozing from her month. Dad fell to his knees, screaming for a nurse, but a second later, Mom sat straight up, giggling with childish mirth. She was the only one who enjoyed that prank. Dad had gone as white as a blank sheet of paper, and I had started blubbering like a baby; we really didn't think it was the least bit funny. I was so scared I got mad. I told her that you shouldn't play jokes like that on children. So she started nibbling me to apologize, and Dad told me that my anger was healthy and wise.

Mom eventually became the boss of the whole third floor. She managed things cheerfully and competently, giving orders, bestowing honors, listening to major grievances and minor complaints, dispensing advice whenever necessary. So one day, Dad brought her a cardboard crown from a Happy Meal, but she laughingly turned it down. "A mad-woman's home may be her castle," she crowed, "but I'm the Queen of the Funny Farm, of the Not Right in the Head, so bring me a funnel or colander crown instead!"

The whole court filed through her chamber every day; it was a ritual. Besotted men—some even wearing suits—came to call, bringing her drawings, chocolates, poems or bouquets of flowers picked on the grounds (roots and all), or they just came to drink in her words. So Mom's room soon turned into a miniature museum and a major mess, with odds and ends everywhere. It was touching, Dad said. He wasn't the least bit jealous of the madmen. When we came into her room, he would clap his hands and all of her Mad Suitors hightailed it out of there, some of them hanging their heads, others apologizing. "See you later, sweethearts," Mom would say, with a regal wave of her hand.

Women called on her, too, though not as many. Most of them came to take tea and to listen to Mom talking about her life before. Their eyes would pop open as they oooh-ed and ahhhh-ed, because Mom's life was so special. The nurses fussed over her, too. Unlike the other patients, she could choose her meals from a menu, leave the lights on as late as she pleased and, what's more, she could even smoke in her room, if she closed the door. We were so thrilled that we started making plans, and forgot all about the moving vans.

Because Mom's head wasn't the only place that the movers were supposed to be emptying out. Our apartment was getting the same treatment. And that move was almost as depressing as the other one. We had to pack centuries of memories into boxes, sort them and throw some away. That was definitely the hardest part. Dad had found a place to rent on the same street, so Mom wouldn't be disoriented when she came home, but it was a lot smaller, so we had to fill a ton of garbage cans. The Creep came to help . . . or so he said, but he wasn't really any help at all. Sometimes he would pull stuff out of the garbage bags and scold us, "You can't throw this out, it could come in handy someday!" undoing the work we'd had so much trouble doing in the first place. It was a pain, because then we had to put stuff in the garbage again, and say good-bye a second time. We couldn't keep everything, there just wasn't enough room at the other place. It was mathematical, Dad said, and he should know. But even I had understood years before that you couldn't get a whole tubful of water into a plastic bottle. It may have been mathematical, but it didn't seem to make horse sense to the Senator.

Dad had been putting on a very brave face ever since Mom had been committed. He was always smiling, and he spent a lot of time with me, talking and playing. He kept up with my history lessons and my art lessons and taught me Spanish with an old tape player that had cassettes that purred as they unspooled. He called me *señor*, and I called him *gringo*, and we tried to have corridas with Mademoiselle, but it never worked. The red rag was like the stopwatch, she didn't give a damn about it. She'd glare at it, lowering her head and twisting her neck, and then she'd run off in the opposite direction. Mademoiselle was a lousy *toro*, but it wasn't her fault, she hadn't been raised that way.

After the living room had been cleaned up, Dad and I repainted the walls. Since the apartment had just been sold, he said I could pick whatever color I wanted. I didn't give a damn though, since we weren't going to live there anymore. But unlike bullfighting, Mademoiselle Superfluous did care about the wall color, so with her help, I chose pond-scum green. We had a good laugh thinking about the owners' faces when they walked into their ugly, depressing new living room.

Dad took me to the movies a lot. That way, he could cry in the dark without my seeing it. I could see that his eyes were red at the end of the movie, but I acted like I hadn't noticed anything. But with the move, he broke down, and started crying in broad daylight—twice. Crying in broad daylight was something else, a whole other level of unhappiness.

The first time, it was because of a photo, the only one Mom forgot to burn. It wasn't even a particularly good one. The Creep had taken it, as you could see, because it showed the three of us plus our mademoiselle crane, sitting on our terrace in Spain. Mom was perched on the guardrail, laughing her head off, while Dad had his hand in front of his mouth, like he was about to cough. My eyes were closed and I was scratching my cheek. Mademoiselle Superfluous was standing next to me, lifting her beak, but with her back to the camera: the whole concept of posing for photos flew right over her head. Everything was out of focus; even the landscape in the background was blurry. It was an absolutely ordinary photo, but it was the last one, the only one that hadn't gone up in smoke. That was why Dad started crying in broad daylight, because all we had left of our good old days was one lousy photo.

The second time he cried was in the elevator after we gave the keys to the new owners. On the fourth floor, we had tears in our eyes from laughing so hard at the hilarious look on the new people's faces. They had walked in on us playing checkers on the tiles in the front hall, with a big bird running every which way and making truly deranged squawking sounds. Their brittle smiles when they thanked us for the scummy, depressing job we'd done on the living room were even funnier. But by the second floor, Dad's laughter had less joy in it, and by the ground floor, the tears in his eyes weren't from laughing anymore. They were tears of true misery. He stayed inside the elevator for a long time, while I waited on the landing outside the closed door.

The new apartment was charming, but not nearly as much fun as the old one. There were only two bedrooms, and the hall was so narrow that we had to hug the walls if we crossed paths in it, and so short that we'd bump into the front door before we'd even picked up speed when we raced. All that was left of the ivy hutch was the ivy; the hutch itself was too big for the living room. With the ivy on the floor and the hutch in the dump, both halves had lost their charm. Trying to fit the big blue overstuffed couch, red club chairs, sand-filled table and city-sticker trunk into the living room meant rearranging everything over and over—a jigsaw-puzzle party that went on for days—before we finally admitted that it wasn't possible. So we banished the sticker trunk to the basement to grow moldy. The big dining table wouldn't fit in either, so we replaced it with a smaller one that wasn't big enough for any dinner guests at all. There was only room for Mom (when she got back), Dad, me and the Creep, who, despite his best efforts, still couldn't balance a place setting on his stomach. I mean, we could put one there—we checked at every meal—but only for a second or two, and then everything would slide off, every time.

In my room, all I had was one medium-sized bed, because if I'd brought the big one—let alone all three—there wouldn't have been a square inch left over for my stuff. We could still play darts with Claude François, but we couldn't back up very far, so the darts all landed smack in the middle of his face. Even Claude wasn't as much fun to play with in that place. The lush, exotic jungle of potted plants in the kitchen had disappeared; now there was just one itsy-bitsy little tub of mint for Dad and the Creep's cocktails.

The bathroom was ridiculously tiny. The Creep could barely even breathe in it. He'd walk in sideways, like a crab, and come out as red as a lobster. We could hear him swearing every time he knocked something over, and afterward, he'd start yelling again because he'd knocked even more stuff over trying to pick the first things up. For him, taking a shower was worse than getting drafted.

As for the poor Prussian cavalier, he was propped up against the wall, with none of the respect due to his rank. He had won tons of battles, his chest was covered in medals, and there he was, plopped on the floor like a vulgar dishrag, with nothing to look at but a rack draped with shabby socks and clumps of wet laundry. That really got me down in the dumps, worse than if I'd had the mumps.

The view from that place was depressing for all of us, for that matter. It faced a courtyard, so there wasn't a lot of sunlight, and we could see the neighbors across the way wandering around their rooms or watching the telly, although they actually seemed to spend more time gaping at the Creep and me playing Russian Droolette or balancing plates on his belly. And at Mademoiselle, who did her vocalizing very early in the morning, waking the whole building up. The minute she opened her beak, the lights in the building all switched on in the blink of an eye.

Mademoiselle was down in the dumps, too. She pecked at the walls as though she wanted to knock them down, making little holes everywhere. She was so bored that she would tuck her head under her wing and go to sleep in the middle of the day. Whether it was Mom's brain or our furniture, no one was really enjoying our moves.

Fortunately, Mom finally got a grip on things. One Friday evening when we arrived at the clinic, the hallways were empty. All the doors were open, but the beds were deserted. There wasn't a single mentally decapitated person in view. Even Air Bubble had floated away. Wandering all over the clinic, we finally heard some noise—music and shouting—coming from the dining hall. When we opened the door, we saw things we had never seen before. All the mentally decapitated people were dancing in their Sunday best. Some of them were slow-dancing in pairs; others gyrated alone, screaming wildly at the top of their lungs. There was even one who was rubbing himself against a pillar and laughing like a regular madman. "Mr. Bojangles" was on replay on the turntable, which had surely never spun for such loony tunes before. Lord knows we had seen some crazy things in our apartment, but this was taking it to another level.

Mom was standing on a table, singing, clapping spoon castanets and stamping her feet like a flamenco dancer, while Sven sat in front of her, playing air piano. They were doing it so well that it really seemed like "Bojangles" was coming out of his hands and her mouth. Even Air Bubble was nodding her head to the rhythm, sitting in a wheelchair and looking more content than I'd ever seen her.

Only Yogurt was upset, because the election had been postponed. He was driving everyone crazy, telling the dancers they had to go vote, because if they didn't, there wouldn't be anyone to govern them the following week. He even tugged at Mom's skirt to try to get her to come down from the table. So she grabbed the sugar bowl that was by her feet and dumped it over his head. Then she called to the other nutcases to help her sweeten Yogurt up. The mentally decapitated all came running over to pour sugar on him, dancing around him like Sioux and chanting, "Sugar for Yogurt, Sugar for Yogurt!"

He just stood there without moving a muscle, waiting to be sweetened, as though there weren't a single nerve in his whole presidential body. Air Bubble watched the whole thing with a big grin, because she was fed up with his presidential nonsense, too. When Mom caught sight of Dad and me, she jumped off the table. Spinning like a top, she whirled over to tell us, "Tonight, my darlings, I'm celebrating the end of my treatment. This whole wretched business is over!"

7.

*P*recisely four years ago, Mom was kidnapped. It was a real shock to everyone at the clinic. The staff couldn't understand what had happened. They were used to patients trying to run away, but they had never had a kidnapping before. Despite the signs of struggle in the room, the window broken from the outside and the blood on the sheets, they hadn't seen or heard a thing. They were terribly sorry, and we were perfectly willing to believe them. Both the patients who had moved out and the mentally decapitated were totally discombobulated. Well, even more than usual, anyway.

Some of them had surprising reactions. The little bald guy with the wrinkly face was 100 percent convinced it was his fault. Crying and scratching his head all day long, he was a truly sorry sight to see. The poor old man tried to turn himself in several times, but anyone could see he was incapable of kidnapping a fly. Another patient was furious that Mom had left without the presents he'd given her. He banged his fists on the walls, cursing her. We were sympathetic at first, but after a while, it really got on our nerves. Insulting my mother was no way to express his sorrow. He even tore up all the drawings he'd given her, which was actually a relief, because that way, we didn't have to bring them back to the apartment. It was bedlam there already.

Yogurt was convinced that a government agency had gotten back at her for demeaning him with the sugar. He kept going up to people to tell them that they'd better not treat him like that anymore, and that the next time anyone was rude to him, the rebels would be kidnapped and tortured. He swaggered around with his chest puffed out and his neck all stiff and straight, like someone who wasn't afraid of anything anymore. To really milk the crisis for everything it was worth, he tried to rally people to his side, but nobody wanted to unite behind His Dairyness. There's a limit to everything.

As for Sven, he pounded his chest, laughing hilariously and pointing at us, then wandered off with his arms flapping, singing in Swedish, Italian or German, we weren't really sure which, but he seemed happy. Then he came back, clapped, pointed to the sky and flew off again, singing some more. Before we left, he gave us a kiss good-bye, scratching our cheeks with his tooth, and splattering us with spittle as he whispered prayers. Sven was far and away the most endearing of the mentally decapitated.

The police couldn't figure out what had happened. They came to examine the room. The window really had been broken from the outside, and the blood really was Mom's. The overturned chair and broken vase indicated that there had been a terrible struggle, but they couldn't find a single footprint in the grass below her window. Their inquiries didn't yield any leads. The staff hadn't noticed anyone acting strangely near the building. The police decreed that we could take the staff's word for it, because noticing people acting strangely was their job.

They questioned us a first time, trying to find out if Mom had any enemies, but we said no—except for a tax assessor, everybody liked her. The tax-assessor lead didn't get them anywhere, so it was soon dropped. They questioned us a second time, but nothing came of that either. Mostly because we had kidnapped Mom ourselves, at her insistence, and even we weren't foolish enough to give evidence against ourselves.

When we got back to Mom's room after the party in the dining hall, she told us in no uncertain terms that she didn't want to live at the clinic anymore. The doctors had told her that she would never be entirely cured, and she didn't want to go on munching pills forever, especially if it wasn't even doing her any good. "Besides, I've always been a little crazy, so a little more or a little less isn't going to change your love for me, right?" Dad and I glanced at each other. We both thought that what she'd said showed real horse sense. Besides, we were tired of coming to the clinic every day, of waiting hopelessly for her to return, of her still-empty place at the table and of our dance parties in the living room that were always getting postponed. There was a multitude of other reasons why things couldn't go on the way they were. Because of the clinic's flaking walls, which made us queasy, and the Bojangles song, which sounded strange in the ward and made us uneasy; because Mademoiselle Superfluous kept making a fuss. And last but not least, because I was starting to get jealous. Of the daft people and the staff people who had Mom with them all day long, unlike us. I was fed up with sharing her, the rest was a blur. We had to undo it, that's all there was to it. I had been thinking that it was criminally negligent to just stand there and wait for the pills to move everything out of Mom's mind, when Dad started to respond, sounding both worried and excited at the same time.

"I totally agree, my dear Verity! We can't allow you to mess with this clinic much longer; the other patients' mental health is at stake! With the excitement and joy you're bringing these lunatics, their mood's going to make big upticks, and then I'll have to worry about your suitors for real! The only problem is that I really don't see how we're going to convince the doctors to release you, or even to decrease your treatment. We're going to have to come up with a real whopper of a lie!" he exclaimed, closing one eye to stare into the hole in his pipe, as though the answer might be inside it.

"George, you happy fool! Haven't we always lived by our own rules? Who said anything about asking permission from some clinic physician? Besides, the best treatment for me would be to be with you two more frequently, instead of spending my time with all these loose screws—they're giving me the blues. If I don't get out of here soon, I'm going to wind up howling at the moon, or hastening my own doom, like the last unfortunate occupant of this room. But I'm not going to let that happen, don't worry. I've figured it all out, but we have to hurry. You two are going to abduct me, that's all there is to it!" Then she clapped her hands with joy, the way she used to.

"Abduct you? You'll have to instruct me. You mean kidnap you, is that it?" Dad asked, choking with surprise, as he fanned the smoke to peer into Mom's eyes.

"That's right, a family kidnapping! I've been preparing it for days. It's a first-rate lie, you'll see. I've figured the whole thing out down to a T. It'll go like clockwork; I haven't left anything to chance!" Mom said, with an excited little dance. She spoke softly, stroking Dad's hair with a conspiratorial air. He seemed lost in thought, his eyes saying, *But, what if . . . ?*, while hers brimmed with excitement at the idea of mischief. His face seemed to thaw, as though he were slowly warming up to her crazy idea. Then, his mind suddenly made up, Dad, who was no slouch when it came to lying, whispered surreptitiously, "Hats off, my dear Reese! This will be your masterpiece! Tell us how you've planned it!" he demanded, as the flames danced over his pipe in a small conflagration, and his eyes twinkled with determination.

Mom really did have everything planned down to the last detail. She had swiped a vial of her own blood the last time they had done blood work. After several nights of observation, she knew that the night watchman left his station every evening at midnight to do his rounds, then stepped out for a smoke on the grounds. That was when we should arrive, she told us. We could stroll right through the front door, as pretty as you please. But Mom really wanted it to be quixotic, you know, so we had to make it look like we'd come in through the window.

Dad and I thought that made sense. Walking out the front door was too mundane for a kidnapping, and even with her pills, Mom still hated anything mundane. If she had wanted to, she could have strolled right out the front door while the watchman was on his rounds, but that wouldn't have been a kidnapping, and it would have wreaked havoc on all her careful planning. At five minutes to midnight, she was going to spill her blood on the sheets, carefully lay a chair on its side and break a vase, using her pillow to muffle the sound. Then she would open the window and smash it—with a towel this time—from the outside, so it would look like a break-in. At five past twelve, we were to show up with stockings on our heads to kidnap her—with her consent—and then we would all tiptoe out the front door for the main event. "What a brilliant plan, my Lulu. So when do you foresee our kidnapping you?" Dad asked, his eyes staring off into the distance, probably trying to rehearse the sequence in his mind.

"When? Why, tonight of course, my darlings! Why wait, since everything's ready? Did you think that party was

happenstance? Oh no, that was my farewell, it didn't happen by chance!"

Back at the apartment that evening, Dad and I rehearsed
the whole mission several times, with a nervous feeling in
the pit of our stomachs. Even though we were scared, we
couldn't help giggling for no reason. Dad looked totally ridiculous with a stocking on his head: his nose was squished
to one side and his lips were even more contorted than usual.
My face was all distorted, too; I looked like a baby gorilla.
Mademoiselle Superfluous was on edge, her head swing-
ing from me to him, trying to understand what was going
on. She craned her neck trying for a better angle, but you
could see it was making her nerves jangle. Before we headed
out, Dad gave me a cigarette and a gin & tonic. He said that
that was what gangsters did before a *real* kidnapping. So he
smoked his pipe, and I, my cigarette, as we sat on the couch,
sipping our libations. Neither one of us said a word, or even
caught the other's eye, so as not to lose our concentration.

I was two sheets to the wind by the time I got into
the car. My mouth was dry, my throat tasted like vomit
and my eyes were stinging, but I felt stronger, too, and I
finally understood why Dad used to drink G & Ts during

his workouts. When we were close to the clinic, we parked away from the streetlights, turned off the engine, and smiled at each other before pulling the stockings over our heads. Even through the stocking, I could see Dad's eyes glowing with a wonderful, veiled light.

Just as we stepped into the clinic, Dad got a run in his stocking, over his nose. He tried to twist it around, but then his ear was sticking out. He kept turning it, laughing quietly and nervously, but the stocking kept running all over his face. Eventually, he just put one hand on the back of his head to hold it in place. We skipped quietly past the night watchman's empty station, then tiptoed quickly to the corner. Before going around it, we pressed our backs to the wall. Dad bent his head around just enough to see if the coast was clear. His chest was bobbing up and down, and he was craning his neck every which way. With all his hocus-pocus, it was pretty hard to focus on the matter at hand. Our trembling shadows loomed before us like a scary reprimand.

Just as we got to the stairwell, I thought we would have to kiss the whole scheme farewell, when I saw the beam of a flashlight sweeping across the wall, and heard the sound of the guard's footfall. I was paralyzed with fear, my feet glued to the floor, but Dad jerked me up by my collar and tossed me into a nook in the hall. Hidden by the darkness, we watched the watchman walk right past us without noticing a thing. By that point, my throat didn't just taste like vomit, it was filled with it, too. I held it in so the noise wouldn't give us away and also because I knew that if I threw up, it would all get stuck in my stocking. After the sound of the footsteps faded away, we charged back to the stairwell like lunatics, dashing up the stairs so quickly that between the G & T and the heebie-jeebies, I thought I really was flying. I had even passed Dad by the second floor.

All we had to do when we got to the third was to storm through the door across the hall. We found Mom sitting patiently on her bloodied bed in the middle of her ransacked room. She had put a stocking over her face, too, but with her masses of hair, it made her head look like a big cauliflower covered in gossamer. "Ah, my sweet captors, my favorite kidnappers, here you are!" she said, speaking low and standing tall. But when she saw Dad's stocking in pieces, she bombarded him with whispers: "Good Lord, George, what did you do to your stocking? You look like a leper! If anyone sees you like that, it will scuttle the whole plan!"

"My nose betrayed me, my Cherie! Come and kiss your knight in shining armor. Show me some ardor, instead of scolding me coldly!" he replied, clasping Mom's hand and drawing her to his side.

As for me, I could barely see. I had the hiccups, sweat was dripping into my eyes, and the stocking was making my cheeks itch. "Our son is drunk!" Mom announced, a bit taken aback to see me staggering. Then she hugged me to her. "Look at this magnificent little hoodlum who swallowed some liquid courage to come and kidnap his mom. Isn't that just the sweetest thing!" she said, as she commenced her nibbling.

"He was perfect," Dad said. "A real gentleman-thief, on the way in, at least. I think he may need some guidance on the way out, though. I do believe that the G & T that I poured so liberally has gone to the poor young man's head."

"Let's soar, freedom is just two flights from that door!" Mom murmured, grabbing my hand in one of hers, and the doorknob in the other. But when she turned it, Sven was standing right outside, making signs of the cross at breakneck speed. So Dad put a finger to his lips, and Sven imitated him, nodding excitedly. Mom deposited a kiss on Sven's forehead, and he kept his index finger on his tooth as he watched us leave.

We raced down those stairs as fast as we could. At the corner, we pressed our backs to the wall once again, and Dad recommended his bobbing and craning until Mom whispered, "George, please stop your clowning around! I already need to pee as it is, and if you don't stop that St. Vitus's dance, I'll laugh so hard I'll wet my pants!" So Dad made one last grand sweep with his arm, to indicate that there was no cause for alarm. Scurrying down the hall, my parents each took one of my hands, and my feet hardly touched the ground as we helped Mom go AWOL.

The atmosphere in the car on the way home was crazy and electric. Dad was drumming on the horn and singing off-key, Mom clapped and laughed, and I watched it all while rubbing my temples, which were pounding mercilessly. Once we had put some distance between us and the clinic, Dad zigzagged all over the road, leaning on the horn as he whizzed around and around traffic circles like they were merry-go-rounds. I slid all over the backseat like a sack of potatoes. When we got home, Dad took champagne out of the fridge, shook it up and sprayed it all over the place. Mom said the new apartment was almost as depressing as the clinic, although it did have more charm. Then she started petting Mademoiselle's head, and as the crane's neck puffed with pleasure, Mom laid out the rest of her plan, gulping champagne to quench her thirst. "I'm going to stay in a hotel until things blow over. It wouldn't look good for anyone to see someone who's been kidnapped swanning out of her own home as pretty as you please. While I'm gone, you'll be cooking up lovely little lies for the police, the clinic and anybody else who asks after me," she explained earnestly, with her glass stretched out like a chalice toward the sacred bottle.

"When it comes to lying, you can count on us, ma'am, we find it quite satisfying. But when the investigation is over, what are we going to do then?" Dad asked, tipping the rest of the bottle into Mom's glass.

"What then? Adventure, my darling little men! The abduction isn't over. But soon we'll be back in the clover. In a few days, when they haven't found me—at least I hope not—we'll go hide out in our Spanish castle in the air. You'll have to rent a car, since I can't fly under the circumstances. We'll take the scenic route to the border, and then we'll drive hell-for-leather to our hideout in the hills. And I'll get back my old life as your doting mom and wife," she said, struggling to stand up and clink glasses with us.

"You really have thought of everything, you're certainly not lazy. How could they ever have thought you were crazy?" Dad wondered, drawing her in for a hug. Catapulted toward sleep by the champagne and the emotions of the evening, I nodded off on the couch watching them do a slow dance with feeling.

While the search for Mom and her abductors was going on, in between our trips to the police station and the clinic to get her things and show off our sad and bewildered faces, we paid her quick visits in a disgusting little hotel where most of the guests paid by the hour. The whores laughed and screamed a lot, often at the same time. Mom had rented her room under an assumed name. "'Liberty Bojangles' is pretty conspicuous for somebody on the run!" Dad observed drily, a teasing smile on his cheeks.

"Au contraire, monsieur, that just shows you don't know a thing about it! Nothing's more discreet in a whorish hotel than an American name. Had you been hiding under a rock until you met me?" she quipped, sashaying around, one hand on her hip, and a finger from the other between her teeth.

"Liberty, with you, I'm a new man every day!" he replied, pulling wads of bills from his pocket. He handed me a few so I could go out for a bit, and asked Mom, "How much?"

The morning of our departure, Mom and I were chatting with the whores and their clients as we waited for Dad to arrive with the rental car. He pulled up in a huge limousine, polished to a mirror sheen, with a silver statuette of a winged goddess on the hood. He parked the car, and when he got out, he was looking good: garbed in gray from head to toe, like a proper British chauffeur. "If Miss Bojangles would care to take her seat," my father said, in an absolutely awful British accent, as he opened the back door with an elegant bow.

"George, you must be out of your mind! This is so conspicuous!" my mother exclaimed, slipping her celebrity sunglasses on and rearranging her fugitive scarf.

"Au contraire, Miss Liberty, that just shows you don't know a thing about it! Going on the run is like lying: the more outrageous the better!" he replied, with a tip of his hat and a click of his heels.

"If you say so, George, if you say so! But I would have loved to cross the border hidden in the trunk of the car. No matter, you may be right, it will be entertaining like this, too," she conceded, once she was seated. Then she waved in response to the admiring whistling and clapping of the whores who had gathered around the car.

Once we were inside, Dad tossed me a child's sailor suit, complete with a silly hat with a pompom on top. Since I refused to put it on at first, he told me that it was what rich American boys wore, that he was in disguise, too, and that if I didn't play along, we would get caught. So I put the awful thing on, and my parents had a good laugh at my expense. Dad was grinning at me like a happy fool in the rearview mirror, and Mom pinched my pompom and crowed, "What an exciting life you lead, my boy! Yesterday you were a gangster, today you're an able seaman! So don't make that face, sweetie, you should be beaming! Just think of your old classmates. Wouldn't they rather be in your place, in a chauffeured limousine? Wherever they are, I'll bet they're not sitting with a Hollywood movie star!"

We took the main road south, because Dad said that with disguises like ours, we didn't need to take the scenic routes anymore. All the cars and trucks honked as they sped by, people waved out the window, and kids massed on the backseats to stare. Three cop cars even passed us, giving us the thumbs-up as they went by. Dad really was the Getaway King. He was right—the more outrageous, the better. Mom was smoking cigarettes and drinking champagne, batting her eyes at admirers as they drove by. "What a career, my boys, what fans! You'd think I'd been doing this since I was a babe. I must be the most famous nobody in the world! George, would you be so kind as to accelerate, the people in the car in front of us didn't have time to wave at me!"

After seven hours of being regally on the run, we stopped at a hotel to spend the night. Dad had booked a suite with a dramatic view over the Atlantic. "Isn't that sweet! I do hope that you remembered to get two rooms: one for my son and I, and one for yourself, my charming chauffeur," Mom announced, thrilled to have the door held open for her, like a real star.

"Of course, Miss Bojangles, a star like you doesn't share a room with the help," Dad replied, leaning into the trunk to extricate our baggage.

In the lobby, all the guests were peeking at us, while trying to look nonchalant, and I was annoyed to note that the staff clearly hadn't seen any rich American boys in sailor suits for a very long time. "A suite for Miss Bojangles and her son, and a room for the chauffeur," Dad requested, having sensibly decided to drop the awful accent. When the elevator door opened, revealing a real American couple, I leapt at the chance to get back at Dad for the sailor suit. Looking down my nose at him, I scolded, "Come, come, George, you can see very well that the elevator's full, please take our luggage up the stairs, so that it won't be in anyone's way." The doors closed on Dad's startled-looking face. The Americans were impressed by so much natural authority in such a young man, and Mom added, "You're right, darling. The help takes such liberties nowadays. Servants are why God—with his keen sense of decorum—invented stairs. It wouldn't do for them to be getting ideas above their station."

The Americans couldn't have understood a word of our haughty nonsense, but they still nodded their agreement. We were laughing our heads off as we waited for Dad, who arrived out of breath and drenched in sweat. With an exhausted grin, he told me, "You're going to pay for that, you little punk. Those three flights with a trunk mean you're going to wear that monkey suit for a month!" But I knew he wouldn't do it. He never held a grudge.

That night, at the fancy hotel's fancy restaurant, I pointed out that this place was more comfortable but less entertaining than the last; things had been a lot livelier with the whores around. Dad explained that there were whores here, too, but they were quieter and more discreet, to fit in. For the rest of dinner, I stared around, trying to unmask the hidden whores, but I wasn't able to. Unlike us, they were quite good at managing not to attract attention.

For our family-reunion dinner, my parents ordered everything on the menu. The table was overflowing with steaming plates of lobster, oysters and scallops served flambé; our glasses were filled with chilled white wine, champagne opened with a sword, red wine and rosé. The waiters hovered around us like hummingbirds, anticipating our every desire. No one in the room had ever seen a meal like that. They even brought in some Russian musicians just to entertain our table. Mom stood on her chair to greet her friends, the stars in the sky, and to dance, swaying to the rhythm of the violins and the shots of vodka.

Dad, on the other hand, sat straight-backed and stiff-upper-lipped, like a true British chauffeur. My stomach swelled up like the Creep's. I didn't even know where to poke my fork anymore, nor how to stop craning my neck this way and that. By the end of the meal, I was seeing stars and whores everywhere. I was tipsy with happiness, and our chauffeur said I was as drunk as a real sailor. For fugitives, we sure did make one heck of a spectacle of ourselves.

Upstairs in the hallway, Mom kicked her stiletto heels so high that they touched the sky—or the ceiling, anyway—and stole my sailor hat. Then she asked me to waltz with her. Her silk scarf caressed my face, and her hands were soft and warm. I couldn't hear anything but her breathing and Dad clapping the beat as he followed us around, dead on his feet, but with a huge grin on his face. Mom had never been so beautiful in her life, and I would have given anything in the world for that song to go on forever. Back in our suite, as I was swallowed up by the down comforter, I felt their arms around me, and knew that they were taking advantage of my tipsy tiredness to move me to the other room.

In the morning, I woke up alone in the chauffeur's bed, and found my parents in the suite, staring at their breakfast with crumpled faces. It was clear that at night, employer and employee had let their guard down and mixed things up, and their relationship had gone all topsy-turvy.

After we checked out at the front desk—where Dad had a coughing fit when Mom paid the bill, leaving fabulous tips for everyone—we drove through the rain on a long straight road lined with tall pine trees that, as Dad said, were nothing to sneeze at. After the party the night before, Mom didn't want to be a star anymore. Every car we passed made her whimper, her head in her hands, "George, please make them stop beeping, or I'll soon be weeping; tell them I'm no star, and to please ignore our car!" But there was nothing Dad could do. If he sped up to leave the cars behind us in the dust, all it did was bring us closer to the ones in front of us.

It was a problem with no solution that was pushing Mom to the brink of an occlusion. I tried not to focus on anything but the road ahead, as through the trees we fled, but it wasn't easy. We were driving forward to get back to our old life, which we were also leaving behind . . . It was hard to picture, but it was also hard to get out of my mind.

Once we left the pine forest, we started climbing into the mountains on roads that twisted and turned all the time. I was focusing on trying not to retch, but I didn't manage that either. Seeing me puke made Mom nauseous, too, and between us we made a terrible mess on my sailor suit and her fancy dress.

As we arrived at the border, the backseat of the car was in total disorder, and up front Dad was as gray as his uniform. The tinted windows were closed, in an attempt to be discreet, even though the car smelled awful, like stale fish and dirty feet. Luckily, there were neither cops, nor customs officers, nor even a gatekeeper or a street sweeper to hamper our passage. Dad said that if nobody bothered us it was thanks to some accord or other, and to the Common Market, but I didn't see what a market, however common, had to do with anything. Even as a chauffeur, Dad could be hard to understand sometimes.

We left our fear at the customs office, and the rain-clouds clinging to the French side of the mountains. Heading down toward the sea beaches, Spain greeted us with bright sun and cool breezes. We opened the windows to get some fresh air, and the mood in the car soon went from fearful to cheerful.

"Wanting to clear out the funk from my drunken sailor and my leading lady, I'm afraid we . . . simply stopped along the way to gather rosemary and thyme. Biding my time, I watched as they sat, sun-dappled beneath an olive tree, laughing and chatting happily. There and then I knew, I would never repent my folly. In my head, a small voice said this was wholly right, I should not get upset, such beauty could not result from poor choice or error. For such wondrous light, there could be no regret. Not ever."

Thus wrote my father in the secret notebooks I found later, afterward.

8.

"*Hysteria. Bipolarity. Schizophrenia.*" *The doctors assailed her with their medical jargon. First they failed her, then they jailed her. They said she was crazy as a jaybird and I raged as they caged her chemically with their medication, and, polemically, with prescription upon prescription, all stamped with that ill-fated inscription: Rx. They caged her far from us, bringing her closer to the cuckoo birds. The object of my dread had now hit us on the head, along with fire and brimstone, right in our own home. Always a live wire, she had actually set our house on fire, attempting to burn away her sorrow with no thought for the morrow. In the innocent haze of happier days I had ignored the countdown, forgotten to track it, but now it was making an incessant racket. Like a disturbingly cracked alarm, an omen of woe and imminent harm; like a siren that makes your eardrums bleed, a barbaric noise that means you need to flee: the party has ended—brutally.*

Yet, at the birth of our son, the contractions seemed to have dispelled some of the stormier, more outlandish aspects of Constance's behavior. Watching her whisper greetings into the ear of our freshly swaddled babe was both beautiful and reassuring. Their very mundanity seemed to be proof of her sanity. Was the ordinariness of caring for a newborn contagious? It seemed to make her less outrageous. During his infancy, he seemed to put a check on her extravagancy. Her wildness seemed more contained, though embers of it still remained. She might say or do things bizarre and unexpected, but her words and acts were inconsequential; to the wider world, her strangeness went undetected.

But the babe grew into a child who toddled and babbled, then walked and talked; a small person—not a bird—who could absorb and repeat all the crazy things he heard. She raised him to be exquisitely polite, because she believed that civility proved your gentility. She taught him that etiquette was the main guardrail in life, and his manners he should mind as a mark of respect due to all humankind. Thus our son bowed and clicked his heels to all and sundry: shopkeepers, distant acquaintances, our demoiselle crane and our copious company. She also taught him to be gallant—in her mind, being chivalrous was never frivolous. She thought a kiss on the hand was an appropriate greeting when meeting little girls *his own age. That made our strolls through parks rather out-dated, charmingly antiquated. It was truly something to see when he scampered across a sandbox to smother a little girl's gritty hand with kisses. They didn't quite know how to react, those flabbergasted little misses. Or the faces of the women at the supermarket, dropping their shopping to gape, as he bowed with deference to express his reverence. Mothers watched him for a while, then—turning back to their own sons, slumped in the carts, drooling and sucking their thumbs—seemed to won-der: were their sons second-rate, or was ours going to wind up a madhouse inmate?*

Our boy's esteem for his mother knew no bounds, and she was so proud that she would have done anything to amaze and amuse him. What most kids do to show off to each other, making and taking dares and double dares, he did with his mother. Endlessly outdoing each other in cheek and imagina-tion, their goal was to inspire each other to shriek in admira-tion, even if that meant turning our home upside down. They jumped, ran, burned, painted, giggled and crowed, eliminat-ing any trace of drabness and filling our lives with cheerful madness. He'd stand before her with a swagger; reaching out a small hand to tag her, "I don't think you can beat me, Mommy, it's terribly risky you see; the winner's sure to be me. So you'd best give up now, since you're bound to lose anyhow!"

"Not a chance, little pup, do you hear me? This mom of yours will never give up, so watch, and cheer me!" Then with one last bounce on the couch, she'd catapult herself over the coffee table and land in a club chair, modestly acknowledging our kudos by patting her hair.

The lad was also endearingly attached to Mademoiselle Superfluous, our pet crane. For a few months, he never let her out of his sight, following her around day and night, imitating her neck movements, walking like her, trying to sleep with his head tucked under his arm, eating what she ate. One evening, we found them sharing a can of sardines in the kitchen, fingers and claws dripping with oil. He would try to get her to play with him, too. "Daddy, Mademoiselle doesn't know how to play right. Can you teach me her language, so I can explain the rules to her?" he asked me one night, as the crane was trampling a board game.

"Talk to her with your hands, your eyes and your heart; that's always the best way to communicate anyway," I replied, without realizing that he would spend whole weeks with one hand over his heart, the other holding the bird's head, so he could stare straight into her great, unblinking eyes.

As for me, I had accepted the role of ringmaster in their

circus, of making their every whim come true, of conducting their boisterous grandstanding while helping them avoid hard landings. Not a day went by without its share of the unexpected, not one evening without an improvised dinner or an impromptu fête.

Coming home from a day's work, I would run into my old pal the Senator in the stairwell, disheveled and sweaty from hauling crates of wine and armfuls of flowers. "Watch out, matey! There's a storm brewing up there, I can feel it in the air! You don't need a weather vane to see it's going to be a real hurricane. We're going to party hearty tonight!" he'd chortle with a look of delight. And I would find my son standing on the landing, doffing his pirate hat as he welcomed our guests, his chin smeared with a coal-black beard, a bandana over one eye, the other wide with pride as he clattered about on a homemade peg leg.

Inside, my lovely wife was clad in silk pirate breeches, her torso emblazoned with a skull-and-crossbones tattoo. Eyes sparkling like buried treasure on tropical beaches, her tapered fingers flew, as she dialed to enlist our friends to empty the last barrels from the hold of this already listing ship. "I've got to go, the captain just showed up. Don't be late—the rum might evaporate!"

Our son would stay up late for those parties, learning to

dance, to use a corkscrew and to shake cocktails. He and the Creep would put silly clothes and makeup on guests who fell asleep on the couch, then take their picture. Our boy would laugh his little head off when the Creep came out of his bedroom stark naked, wailing that he wanted to drown himself in a barrel of vodka. Together they had come up with a clever stratagem to lure both misses and missuses into the Senator's lair. The Creep would discreetly designate his chosen belle for that night's ball, and our son would materialize at her side, looking as innocent as a choirboy, offering her all sorts of colorful libations. Not wanting to hurt such a sweet little lad's feelings, they accepted the drinks, unaware of the high jinks, until their heads were reeling.

That was when the Creep would come over and start boasting about his latest mission, his meetings with the president and the advantages of knowing a man in his position. Then, sucked in by his game, they'd follow him to the bedroom, where he fed them tidbits of power and crumbs of fame. One night, our son, having probably come to the conclusion that it was time to go into business for himself, managed to attract a lovely lady into his own room. He unbuttoned his shirt, took his little pants off and tossed his mini long johns aside, then started jumping up and down on the bed, naked as a newborn baby before the totally charmed, slightly flattered, and perhaps somewhat alarmed young lady.

All in all, it's no real surprise that our offspring's more formal education didn't go as well as we'd hoped. Spending his evenings in the company of financial titans and defrocked monks, listening to the alcohol-fueled diatribes of inspired drunks, joining their overheated debates and excited confabulation must have made his schooldays and schoolmates appear rather dull and drab in relation.

To be honest, "days" is something of an exaggeration; "half days" would be more like it. After those late nights, we kept him home almost every morning. When Marine and I would show up, somewhat green around the gills, our eyes hidden behind dark morning-after glasses, fishing for an absurd new excuse every day, the teacher would stare at us—at first in dismay, then with less and less hope.

Once, at the end of her rope, she blew up, yelling, "He can't just waltz into school any time you two please!" To which my charming Louise, high as a kite, retorted with a touch of spite, "Well that's too bad, because learning to waltz would at least be useful, unlike anything else you're teaching him at this silly school. You give him children's books, when at home he discusses great literature with authors and politicians, lays traps with ease for tipsy chickadees, debates the finer points of

Newton's Law and global finance with international bankers and prizewinners in science. He courts women, from common to Brahmin, and you expect us to care about what time he comes in? What do you want him to grow up to be—a pencil-pushing desk jockey? My son is a highbrow night owl, and you want to turn him into an oil-slicked gull in a sea of ennui! That's why he shows up at noon, so don't expect to see him in the morning any time soon!"

I stood there, mildly amused, as she unleashed that torrent of zany zings, while our son hung back, fanning the air with his imaginary highbrow night-owl wings. After that umpteenth skirmish, I knew our son's schooldays were numbered. The solution would have to be homeschooling, as his teacher's good will was rapidly cooling.

He thought it was just a game, so our little boy watched it all with joy. Convinced his mother was pretending, he didn't realize her crazy act was never-ending. He thought it was just a game, so I acted as if I thought the same. No matter how out of line she'd get, I tried not to look too surprised or upset.

But one night, after a quiet day spent reading, Colette took off her glasses and rubbed her nose, then asked me, in a voice both fretful and pleading, "Pray tell me, monsieur—and please hurry—what's going on, so I won't have to worry. It says right here in this book—I can show you if you'd like to have a look—that Josephine Baker left Paris during the war. I don't want to be a bore, but if it's true, then consequentially, you couldn't have run into her so providentially! Wherefore all the deceit and falsehood? You can't be my grandfather, my good man. Either they've recorded the dates just anywise, or it's all one big tissue of lies! This is impossible, it simply can't be! Impossible, impossible, do you hear me? As it is I don't have a name of my own, and now this book is whittling my family tree down to the bone! What will be left of me? How do I know if you're really my spouse? Why do we even live in the same house? Will the next book I read prove that Dracula is no relation of yours? I'm so topsy-turvy I can't tell the doors from the floors!"

For once her plea betrayed not a shred of fantasy; the distress in her voice had nothing to conceal: it was real. This, sadly, was no lark; her eyes had gone dark, as though turned inward, watching her world implode. Feeling the ground shift beneath my feet, I sensed imminent defeat.

While our son giggled hilariously and scribbled a family tree that no one could make head nor tails of, Colette peered at me with neither hatred nor love—only curiosity, nothing more, like when you pass someone in the street and wonder where you've seen them before. Jabbing a finger at me, and with fur-

rowed brow, I could see that she was lost to me now. Her head lolled, and as she trolled secret spells, I got the impression she was shaking herself gently to try to get things back into place and recover her sanity. "I have to go lie down for some bits, I'm at the end of my wits; I'm feeling bamboozled with all of your trumpery," she said somewhat grumpily, as she headed to bed, looking calm, her head tipped to one side, watching her left thumb trace the lines on her right palm.

"So who is Mom again, actually? Can you explain it to me factually? She's my grandmother, is that it? And Josephine Baker is my great-grandmother? It's kind of a pain: our tree doesn't fit the stencil, it's all treetops, but no branches," our son complained, chewing on his pencil.

"You know, son, your mom's got lots of imagination. She fiddles with everything, even her filiation. But in your tree, Mom is your roots, your leaves, your branches and your tree-top all at once, and we are her gardeners. So we're going to do our best to keep our favorite tree standing upright, and not let it get uprooted, all right?" I replied, wrapping a muddled metaphor in faux gusto. He decided to accept the mission, albeit dubitatively, then retired to his room, muttering ruminatively.

After the fire though, there was no way to pretend it was a joke. The sound of the sirens, the billowing smoke. Madness may be in the eyes of the beholder, but it was no longer possible to ignore the sadness lurking behind her surges of rapture. I watched as my son covered his mom with the shiny survival sheet, pulling it up over her shoulders reflectively, hiding the puddles of plastic and flaky ashes. He pulled it up so he wouldn't see, couldn't see, the burned stigmata of his childish insouciance going up in smoke.

He displayed tremendous self-control throughout the ordeal, staying stiff-lipped and focused while his mother was questioned, first by the police and then the doctors. He never yielded an inch, not once did he flinch; not a single tear ran down his proud, composed face. Nothing betrayed his misery except his arms, stiff from jamming clenched fists into his pockets. His visage remained serious and focused as he analyzed the situation.

Still, when he learned that, in addition to being slightly burned, his mother was being interned, he slashed at the air with his foot, exclaiming, "We're in a real pickle, but we're going to find a way out, right, Dad? Life can't just go on without her! We've got to find a way to give our troubles a kick in the butt!"

Going home alone with him that night, I decided he was right. I spared him the unbearable truth, and told him that the doctors had said that after plenty of rest in bed, his mom would come home someday, just not right away. In the meantime, we would do our bit by visiting her every day. They had said no such thing. For them, her condition was clearly worsening. That depressing mental ward was all we could look forward to. I had to lie; I couldn't bear to tell our son that to spare other people's lives, that was where his mom would have to die.

Walking down the street on that lovely spring night, I was no longer the "happy fool" I had prided myself on being for so long. The first word in my title was gone, but for my son's sake, I would have to carry on. When I met his mother, I had made a major wager. I'd read the rules, signed the contract, accepted the conditions and clauses and initialed all the pages. I didn't regret a thing. How could I regret that sweet wackiness, all that thumbing our noses at reality, those birds flipped at convention, clocks and seasons, at how things are supposed to be? At this point, there really was nothing left to do but to give rhyme and reason a kick in the butt, too. So I added one more clause to the contract. After years of frenetic festivities and esthetic inebriety, poetic eccentricity and kinetic gaiety, I couldn't see myself telling my son that all the fun was done, from here on in, we would watch his mother drowning in madness in a loony bin. That she was mentally ill and not even the strongest pill could keep her afloat. So I lied, so as not to rock his boat.

Molly's condition was unstable. We never knew what state we'd find her in, so every time we went to see her, I could sense our little boy's chagrin, wondering if, when we got there, her private weather would be foul or fair. The pills they gave her provided some relief, helped her turn over a new leaf. Often she seemed like before, pleasantly loopy, though her eyelids were somewhat more droopy. But other times, when we opened the door, we found her conversing with her demons or rehearsing with phantoms, head bowed in prayer, reciting psalms she composed according to her own axioms. Within a few days, she had become the center of the maze; staff and patients alike adored and pampered her, called her "m'lady" and spoiled her like crazy.

Our son soon learned to make his way around the labyrinth of hallways where lost souls knocked around inside bodies wandering all ways. Somehow he found his marks, performed his rounds. You could even say he had some friends, in that surreal world without end. First he'd hold forth with a music-loving schizophrenic, then test his bedside manner on a criminally insane woman rendered harmless through neurogenics.

His mom and I took advantage of his being out of the room to plot her jailbreak, a getaway worthy of the Great Escape, which we had christened "Operation Liberty Bojangles." Molly was very enthusiastic about it, pointing out that if I were committed to the clinic, too, I wouldn't feel out of place, I would be just another nutcase. "George, honey, you're looking a bit morose. I would share my pills with you, but I've already swallowed my whole dose," she said through a medicinal haze. "But tomorrow, I promise, I'll leave some behind. You can't tell me that Operation Liberty Bojangles is the product of a sound mind!"

Operation Liberty Bojangles was the kick in the butt our son had insisted we give our troubles. I couldn't resign myself to bringing the novel of our lives to an end without a dramatic, quixotic twist, even if it meant bending reality yet again. We had to give our son a final chapter in the style to which he was accustomed: a plot bursting with surprises, joyful and overflowing with love and affection. Molly wanted to take responsibility for this final folly; the kidnapping stratagem was actually a diadem, crowning her, in absentia, Queen of the Loony Bin. She just wanted to amaze and amuse her son one last time. She did it for him, that's all.

9.

$\mathcal{A}$ towering pine had always stood in front of the terrace, shooting up from some thirty feet below. In years when we spent the holidays in Spain, it would be our Christmas tree. We'd spend whole days on the decorations we'd bestow. With a tall ladder, we draped it in glittering tinsel and twinkling lights, strewed it with cotton snow. At the very top, a giant star would go. It was a majestic tree, and decorating it had always filled us with glee. But, like everyone, it had grown. From the moment that the castle became our hideout, Mom had been railing that it blocked the sun and spoiled the view. It kept us from seeing the lake, and if a big storm blew up one night, it would fall and break through the roof, killing us in our beds. As far as she was concerned, an assassin was looming right over our heads. She talked about it whenever it caught her eye, and since you could see it from every window, it was constantly in her line of vision. The tree didn't really bother

Dad or me; we could step around it easily for a view of the lake that was still great. But for Mom, it had become an obsession, and leaving it there was out of the question. Because the tree wasn't actually on our property, Dad had to go into town, and ask the mayor for permission to cut it down. But the mayor said no, leave it be. If everyone cut down every tree that blocked a view, there'd be no more forest, then what would they do? On our way home, Dad said that he agreed with the mayor in theory, but that what with Mom so teary, we had to find a way to make her feel okay. I really didn't know what to think: choosing between making Mom happy and saving the forest was enough to make you need a drink.

Aside from the Creep, who still spent his senatorial vacations with us, playing Russian Droolette with me, working on achieving success by growing his belly, and grilling sausages on the terrace, we had no more company. The first time the Creep came, he drove Mademoiselle Superfluous down with him. He arrived in a state of advanced physical and morale fatigue. Mademoiselle had screeched and squawked the whole way, flapping her wings, tapping her beak against the windows and turning the backseat into one huge crap table. To make matters worse, Customs had given him a hard time at the border. They'd inspected everything: his papers, his car, his luggage . . . and they'd started all over when he'd insisted he was a senator, since they assumed they were dealing with an imposter.

Getting out of the car, he decreed that he never wanted to see Mademoiselle again, not ever, and if it were up to him, he'd roast her on a spit, and eat her all by himself, washing her down with a good bottle of Bourgueil. As for Mademoiselle, she dashed straight to the lake and spent the rest of the day down there sulking. After the Creep went back to Paris to his job in Luxembourg Palace, it was just the four of us, and that was fine with us.

Sometimes Dad would call the police to see how the investigation was going. He'd put the loudspeaker on so Mom could hear the cop tell us that they still hadn't found her. We clapped our hands over our mouths, laughing silently, as Dad raged, overacting defiantly, "This is unbelievably awful! How can you let her abductors get away with anything so unlawful?"

Then, taking a deep breath to pull himself together, he'd say mournfully, "There's a little boy here who needs his mother. Are you sure you've got no leads at all?" The cop's answer was always the same: sounding ashamed, he would say he was glad that my father had called, but admit that the investigation had stalled. As soon as Dad hung up, I would quip, "If the investigation is stalled in Paris, they're not going to catch up with us any time soon! It took us long enough to get here in a vehicle that ran, so if theirs is stalled, they won't be here for a really, really long time." That always cracked my parents up.

Every morning, while Dad and I were still asleep, Mom would go swimming in the lake with Mademoiselle Superfluous to keep her company. She would dive off the rocks, then float on her back, watching the sun rise. Mademoiselle would wade around her, squawking and trying to catch fish in her beak, but she never could. After all that time, she had turned into a lap bird who ate canned tuna fish, enjoyed classical music, wore custom-made jewelry, attended cocktail parties and had lost the knack for birdier things.

"I love staring up at the wild blue yonder while listening to the marine sounds from deep under. It really carries me away. What better way to start the day?" Mom would comment when she got back. Then she'd make us a delicious breakfast, with homegrown orange juice, the best we'd had in our lives, and honey that came from the neighbor's hives.

After breakfast, we'd go to the markets in all the little villages near the house, a different market in a different village every day of the week. I was on a first-name basis with all the vendors, and lots of times they would give me free fruit. Sometimes it was bags of whole almonds that we'd break open with a stone or the heel of a shoe. When we didn't know how to cook their fish, the fishmongers would tell us what to do. And the butchers would give us Spanish recipes, like pork in a salt crust, mayonnaise with garlic, or really crazy paellas with fish, meat, rice, peppers and everything else all thrown in at once. Then we'd go sit and sip coffee in one of those plazas where everything was painted white and gilded with strong sunlight.

Dad would snort as he read the newspaper, because it was a crazy world, and Mom would ask me to tell her fabulous stories as she smoked, eyes closed and face turned toward the sun, like a sunflower. When I ran out of ideas, I would describe what we'd done a day or two before, adding a few little falsehoods. Usually those tall tales were every bit as good as my entirely made-up stories.

After lunch, we'd let Dad think about his novel, lying in the hammock with his eyes closed, while we went down to the lake for a swim if the weather was warm, or to pick big bouquets of wildflowers and skip stones on the water if the air was cool. When we got back to the house, Dad had gotten a lot of work done; you could tell by his puffy face and all the ideas and cowlicks in his hair. We'd put "Bojangles" on at high volume for cocktail hour, before grilling something for dinner. Then she'd switch to some livelier tunes, and Mom taught me to dance: rock 'n' roll, jazz, flamenco and more. She really knew how to rock the floor. Every night before turning in, I was allowed to smoke one cigarette, to practice making smoke rings. We'd make a bet, and as we watched the rings rise high and evaporate into the starry sky, we'd savor every puff of our new lives as fugitives.

Unfortunately, after a while, the moving vans started showing up in Mom's brain now and again. Brief moments of madness that popped up in the blink of an eye. They lasted twenty minutes or an hour, and then, just like that, they were gone again, in nothing flat. For weeks, there'd be no sign of them. While she was on one of her mad tears, the pine tree wasn't her only obsession—anything could stoke her crazed aggression. One day, she wanted to smash all our plates, because the sun reflecting off of them had dazzled her, and she suspected them of trying to make her go blind. Another day she wanted to burn all of her linen clothing, because it was burning her skin. She swore there were blisters on her arm that we could neither see nor feel, but she scratched them all day until they bled for real.

Another time she was sure that the lake was poisoned, just because after a hard rain one night, the color of the water had changed. The next day, she would swim in the lake and dine off the porcelain plates, garbed in her linen clothes, filling our ears with her upbeat chatter, as though nothing had ever been the matter. When the tide turned again, she would take us as her witnesses, wanting to prove her hallucinations were true. Dad would try to calm her down and show her that she was mistaken, but there wasn't a thing he could do. She would get all worked up, screaming and gesticulating, leering at us with a horrifying smile and resenting our lucidity. "Why don't you understand; how can you not see it when it's as plain as the nose on your face!"

She didn't usually remember what she'd done afterward, so Dad and I never talked to her about it. We acted like nothing had happened, figuring there was no point in rubbing salt in her wounds. Those occasions had been hard enough to get through once; who needed to relive them a second time? Sometimes though, she realized that she had gone too far, had said and done awful things. That was worse, because at those times, we weren't scared of her, we just felt bad for her, terribly, terribly bad. She would try to wash away her sorrows with tears, and it seemed like she would never be able to stop crying, like when you've picked up too much speed to stop running down a hill. Her sorrows fell on her from somewhere very, very high, and there was no way she could stand up to them. Her makeup couldn't stand up to them either. It scattered from her eyelids and eyebrows, running all over her face, smearing her plump cheeks, trying to flee her terrified eyes, which made her so frighteningly beautiful. When the wave of sorrow ebbed, the depression flowed back in, and she would sit in a corner, hair hanging in front of her face, head slumped, legs jiggling nervously. She'd be panting, trying to catch her breath as though she'd just run a race. I figured she was probably trying to stay ahead of her sadness, that's all. Dad and I felt totally useless when she was in that state. Try as he might to soothe or reassure her, or I to beguile her into smiling, when she was like that, nothing worked. She was inconsolable. There was no room for us between her and her problems, there wasn't even any air; they took up all the space that was there.

To lessen the scope and shorten the duration of those crises, the three of us agreed it was time for an intervention.

So we discussed what we could do to lessen her trials and tribulations. Dad suggested that Mom stop drinking cocktails day and night. He loved cocktails too, he said, but perhaps drinking them all the time wasn't good for what ailed her. Though the cocktails weren't necessarily speeding up the move, they probably weren't slowing it down, either. Mom agreed, but with a heavy heart, because cocktails were a big part of her life. She did negotiate a glass of wine every night with dinner, to start the evenings feeling like a winner.

Like a criminal turning herself in, she would ask us to lock her in the attic at the very first signs of an attack. She explained that she didn't know why, but only in the dark could she look her demons in the eye. With infinite sadness, Dad agreed to sweep out the cobwebs and move some furniture up there, so that she could stay in her aerie as long as necessary. You have to love someone very much to lock them in such a horrible place, to leave them there in the dark. Every time she started to get fanatic, Dad raged inside at having to put her in the attic. But the louder she screamed, the more quiet-spoken he became, and he kept his word, though it broke his heart. I would cover my ears to try not to hear her.

If it went on too long, I'd go down to the lake to make

my head clearer, and to try to forget about all the nasty surprises life seemed to have in store for us. But sometimes, even at the lake, I could hear the terrible chorus. So I would sing until her screams faded to whispers.

Once she had won the battle against her demons, the combat against herself, she would knock gently at the door and emerge from the ransacked attic, looking victorious, exhausted and somewhat inglorious. Even though those struggles in the attic required all of her might, she still couldn't sleep at night, so she needed pills. Fortunately, the demons never came when she slept; sleep provided an escape from her woes, offering her some well-earned warrior's repose.

Since Mom couldn't have cocktails in the evening anymore, Dad would go drink his outside with the pine tree. Wearing rubber boots, and standing amongst the roots, his own drink he sipped, while from a watering can, a toxic mix slowly dripped. When I asked him why he had started having cocktails with the tree, he came up with a whimsical story. He told me that he and the tree were drinking to the pine's upcoming liberty. It would soon be free to sail the seven seas, because one night, when he hadn't even been drunk, pirates had called to say they wanted that particular trunk for the mast of their ship. Rather than hacking at it with an ax, he was helping it fall more gently . . . and covering his tracks. "You see, my son, this tree has won the right to visit exotic ports, and face down terrible storms. It will sometimes be becalmed, before the winds help it sail on. It will travel the world, all sails unfurled. Flying a skull-and-crossbones flag, it will soon be able to brag of a thousand adventures far more exciting than standing here waiting to be hit by lightning!" Then with an offhand toss, he poured the last toxic drops into the moss.

I wondered how in the world he could come up with such malarkey. I knew perfectly well that he was having drinks with the tree for Mom's sake, to help her see the lake. He hoped that with his toxic mixture, the tree would soon be out of the picture, and that with it gone, perhaps Mom's mind might be less forlorn. But when I started dreaming about the ship sailing from the Mediterranean to the Caribbean, and about the pirates on board, cheerfully counting the gold and treasure in their hoard, I could better measure what a worthy story it was. As ever, he told such beautiful lies for love.

When she wasn't turning herself in to be locked up, Mom was more and more thoughtful toward us. Every day, on her way back from her morning swim, she'd pick little bouquets that she'd set on the tables by our beds. Sometimes there'd be a little note, too—a line from a book she liked, or one of her own beautifully crafted poems. All day long she'd be wrapped in Dad's arms, or else she'd wrap me in hers. Every time I'd walk by her she'd grab my hand and pull me toward her chest to listen to her heartbeat, and to whisper compliments in my ear.

She'd talk about when I was a baby, about the party filled with mirth they'd had in her room at the clinic to celebrate my birth, and how the other patients had been irate about the music and the noise that went on 'til late; about the times she had danced all night long to rock me to sleep; how the first steps I took were to try to grab at the crest atop Mademoiselle's head, and how the first lie I told was to accuse Mademoiselle of having wet my bed; and also just plain about how happy it made her to spend time with me. She had never talked like that before, and I really liked when she told me stories about things I couldn't remember, although even I could realize that there was more melancholy than joy in her eyes.

10.

To celebrate the feast of San José, the people of the village organized a fiesta that lasted all day. They started in the morning by dressing a huge wooden Virgin Mary in bouquets of flowers; that took several hours. Whole families would show up with armfuls of red and white roses, leaving their offerings at the foot of the statue. Then the organizers would arrange them so cleverly that right before your eyes, they garbed the statue in a red dress with a white pattern and a white cape with a red one. Although I was watching the whole time, I still couldn't tell how it was done. In the morning, there was nothing but a head on a wooden skeleton, and by evening, there was the Virgin Mary, all decked out for the party in a beautiful, sweetly scented dress, like a real princess.

All day long, firecrackers had been going off all over the place, rumbling and grumbling up and down the valley. At first it startled me, because it sounded like a war movie, but nobody else seemed bothered, so I decided not to worry. Dad told me that Spaniards partied like soldiers, but I had never seen a battle like that, bursting with flowers, firecrackers and sangria.

Over the course of the day, the streets began to fill up with families garbed in traditional clothes. People came from all over the valley, and even further afield. From granddads to granddaughters, they all looked like they'd stepped out of a picture book; even the babies had colorful gowns for their big night out on the town.

Mom had bought us costumes that followed local custom. Unlike the sailor suit Dad had gotten me, I was happy to put on the shiny vest, baggy trousers and white moccasins, because you never feel ridiculous when you can blend in with the crowd. Mom had tamed her crazy hair with a black lace mantilla, and, for a new look, had slipped into a gown with a big puffy skirt, like a queen in a history book. The outfit made her so warm that she had to keep fanning herself with a black fan with butterflies embroidered on it. She fluttered the fan so quickly that it looked like they would fly away any minute.

During the afternoon, the streets filled with Spaniards parading religiously, because for them, the fiesta was something they took seriously. They looked proud and happy, and I thought that with parties like that, they had every right to be. When night fell, the streets lit up with bonfires and torches to illuminate the dancing and merrymaking. On the square in front of the church, at the foot of the Virgin Mary, the townspeople had cooked a paella in a dish so big that you needed long wooden rakes to reach the rice simmering in the middle. Everybody helped themselves, and sat to eat wherever they pleased, because the fiesta was like a paella—a carefully dosed blend of this, that, and everything else, all mixed together.

When the meal was over, they celebrated by setting fireworks off all over the place: from the rooftops, the mountains in the distance, the boats on the lake; there was banging and booming and colorful starbursts shooting into space. The walls were splattered with bursts of light, and by the end, the sky was so bright that you could barely tell if it was day or night. In fact, for just a moment, hardly more, the darkness had a total eclipse, and across from me I glimpsed Mom's face. Tears streamed down from her eyes to her lips, then curved inwards, toward her proud, trembling chin, before leaping to the ground. Through it all, she never made a sound.

When the fireworks were over, a tall, striking woman in a red-and-black dress climbed to the top of the church steps and began to sing love songs from the heart of a small orchestra. To help her words soar higher, she raised her hands to the sky. Her voice was so beautifully sad that we wondered if she was going to start to cry to give it even more emotion. But instead, she switched to happy songs that started a commotion. Everyone clapped to the rhythm as they danced. The atmosphere was magical: I was totally entranced. Like marionettes, the silhouettes spun and darted; not one single person looked brokenhearted. Skirts billowed out in a haze of bright hues, as dancers leapt and twirled, floating in their own magical world.

With her dress of lights and lace, big dark eyes and olive-skinned face, one of the girls was like a perfect doll, and I confess that I was in her thrall. I couldn't wrench my eyes away: her hair, her smile, her pink cheeks, I could have stared at her for weeks. She fanned her face gently, smiling intently, yet there seemed to be an ocean between her and me. Still, I stared at her for so long that by and by, eventually I caught her eye. When she looked at me, I went weak in the knee, losing all track of time as a shiver ran up and down my spine.

Shortly before midnight, the crowd opened up a small space before the stairs, so the dancers could take their place in pairs. One by one, the couples danced an homage to the singer and her entourage. First came the elderly ones, with fragile bones and years of experience. Old as they were, they showed no weariness. Their movements were smooth and practiced, the decades had taught them certain tactics, they danced and spun as everyone applauded, and when they were done, by the crowd they were lauded.

Then younger couples stepped up to show off their high spirits and ardor. They whirled and twirled harder and harder, until you might have thought their colorful clothes were about to burst into flames, as the crowd clapped and chanted their names. As they danced, the gals and the guys stared into each other's eyes with a strange blend of domination and admiration, topped off with smoldering passion.

There were also couples that spanned generations, which was just so sweet: little boys treading on grandmas' feet, little girls twirling in their fathers' arms, knowing they wouldn't come to any harm. They were clumsy, approximate and affectionate, and though none of them danced imperiously, they all took their turn quite seriously. Like anything done with attention and application, it deserved our appreciation, so everyone clapped quite loud when they bowed.

Then out of the blue, I saw Mom heading for the dance floor, one hand on her hip and the other upturned toward

Dad. Although she seemed to be in good cheer, I was instantly filled with fear. With so much at stake, I knew they couldn't make a mistake. Dad entered the arena with chin held high, and through the crowd ran a sigh. Though they said nothing out loud, the atmosphere was electric, as the townspeople settled in to watch the eccentrics—the only people for miles around who hadn't grown up near this little town. For me, it was both exciting and stressful.

After what felt like ages, the orchestra began to play, and my parents, like felines released from their cages, started circling each other, eyes locked, my mother's movements light as a feather. My father's eyes couldn't tame her, but his love and support became her. I could have sworn I heard him say, "Come, my beloved, let's fly away."

Then the lady in red began to sing, the guitars woke up, the cymbals started to ring, the castanets clattered and chattered, and my head felt light as my parents began to soar through the night. They spun and twirled higher and higher, leaping like flames in a bonfire. Their feet off the ground and their heads in the air, they'd touch down for an instant, then fly back up on a dare. Like impatient whirlwinds they spun ecstatically, their incandescent passion lighting up the scene dramatically.

I had never seen them dance so fiercely, it was like a

first dance, and a last one, too, but they weren't done; it was a beginning, a middle and an end all in one. That dance was like an insane prayer, as though no one else were there.

They danced without breathing, and yet they went on, and I hardly exhaled for the length of the song. I didn't want to miss an instant of this bliss, nor to forget a single wild step. They poured their whole lives into that performance—the bad and the good, huge torrents of passion, folly and love—and the townspeople clearly understood. When it was over, they clapped like crazy for the foreigners who were anything but lazy. As my parents bowed, to the singer, the orchestra and then the crowd, applause for their grand finale echoed throughout the valley. Proud of them and hugely relieved, I finally felt like I could breathe. As on my feet I did sway, I was almost as exhausted as they.

After the applause, which was deafening, everyone to them was beckoning, so my parents did the rounds, drinking sangria with half the town. I let them revel in their newfound glory, an unexpected new chapter in their love story. I stayed out of the limelight, sipping a soft drink, wanting only to think about my Spanish doll, my belle of the ball, who through it all, still had me in her thrall. Since all the girls wore the same dress, I searched for her without success. Or rather, I saw her everywhere, in a smile, a lock of hair. In the end, it was she who came up to me, her face hidden by her fan, the hem of her billowy dress in one hand.

She spoke without looking at me directly, in Spanish that I couldn't really understand correctly. She talked and talked, the words rising from the back of her throat, the R's rolling off of her tongue, while I looked as dumb as a goat: my jaw hung, and I gaped like a fish out of water. Yet she sat down next to me and kept on talking for both of us, because she could see that I was utterly useless. She didn't ask a single question, I could tell from her intonation—she carried both sides of the conversation, occasionally glancing at my face, still like a fish's. If I'd had three wishes, one of them would have been for our chat to go on like that forever. She shared her thoughts and the breeze from her fan; occasionally she'd pause, and then, with a smile, launch in again.

In the midst of all that bliss, she stopped midsentence to give me a kiss—on the lips, as though she were my wife. I'd never been so happy in my life. So what did I do? I was immobile, a real imbecile. I'm kind of ashamed to have been so lame. She laughed and left, and then, with a swish of her petticoat, turned back to see the face of her freshly hooked fish, still dumb as a goat.

As soon as we got home, I went to bed, but soon after I had turned out the light, while I was still lying awake rerunning the film of that incredible night in my head, I heard the door open gently, and saw Mom's silhouette come soundlessly toward my bed. She lay down beside me, and curled me in her arms, as if to guide me. Believing I slept, she briefly wept, then started to speak, low and slow. Eyes closed, I listened, feeling her warm breath in my hair, just enjoying her being there.

In a hushed whisper, she told me the story of a family that was ordinary, and of a charming and intelligent little boy who was his parents' pride and joy. The story of a family that, like any family, had its ups and downs, but overall, more smiles than frowns. Most importantly, they loved each other and lived in harmony. Of a wonderful, generous dad, who rolled his bulging blue eyes and rarely got mad, and did everything in his power to make every hour as merry as could be.

But sadly, a crazy disease had wormed its way to the heart of that jolly tale, and begun to assail their carefree life. Choking back sobs, Mom murmured that she had figured out a way to lift that curse before it got any worse. In a hoarse whisper, she said that it would be better, I'd see, and I believed her instinctively. It was a relief for me to know that we would soon get back to how it used to be, before her madness brought us so much sadness. She traced the sign of the cross on my forehead, then kissed me before she rose from my bed. As soon as Mom closed the door, I drifted off, confident that things would soon go back to how they'd been before.

11.

The next morning, on the table on the terrace, a magnificent bouquet—mimosa and lavender, rosemary, poppies,
and oleander—towered over the breakfast tray. Leaning
over the guardrail to look at the lake, I saw Mom floating
on her back like she did every morning, her white tunic
fanned out around her, her eyes toward the blue yonder,
her ears tuned to the sounds from deep under, because as
she liked to say, there was no better way to start the day.

Turning around, I saw Dad, fresh from the shower, grinning at all the flowers. But sitting down, his grin quickly
turned into a frown when he spied a pile of emptied-out
sleeping pills. He glanced at me, his eyes filled with fright,
then leapt up and ran down to the lake at the speed of
light. I froze, sensing I had to beware, but unwilling to understand what was going on down there. I watched Dad
run, watched Mom float in the sun, her arms forming a
cross, her dress as white as an albatross as she drifted away

from the shore. I watched Dad dive in and swim out, then I didn't want to watch anymore.

Once he'd carried Mom out of the lake, Dad laid her on the beach. He tried to revive her, touching her everywhere, pounding her chest like a madman, kissing her to share his air, show her his love and feelings. I don't remember going down and yet somehow I was next to him, looking grim, holding Mom's icy hand as he kissed her and whispered. He spoke as if she could hear him, as if she were alive, as if she would survive. He told her he understood, that he would do what he could, that everything would be okay, it was just a bad day, that maybe not this afternoon, but they would be together again soon. And Mom just let him talk, looking very wise, she knew that what he said was lies, that everything was over and done, that there would be no more fun. Mom's eyes stayed open so as not to add to his misery, because sometimes lies are gentler than reality.

But I knew that this was the end, I had lost my best friend, because echoing in my head were the words she had murmured last night in my bed. And I cried, I cried like never before, I cried because I was so mad at myself for not having opened my eyes last night, for not having made things all right. I cried from regret—why hadn't I grasped any sooner that her awful solution was to bid us farewell, to disappear, so we wouldn't have to hear the screams in the attic anymore, or the static in her mind when she couldn't find a way to be kind?

I was crying because I had understood too late, that's all. If only I had opened my eyes, if only I had replied, if I had asked her to stay with me, told her that, crazy or no, we loved her so, she might have been brave and not floated to her grave. But I hadn't said a word, hadn't even stirred, and now here she was, her body already cold, impossible to hold, her eyes far away, not seeing our fears, her ears already deaf to our tears.

The three of us stayed by the lake for a long time, so long that Mom's hair and her long white gown had time to dry. With the wind, her hair swayed; with the wind, her face seemed less dismayed, more alive. She was staring up at the sky to which she had flown. Her eyes were veiled by her long lashes, her lips parted. Her hair dancing in the wind made us feel less chagrined. The three of us stayed by the lake for a long time, because that was the best place for us to be, all three, looking at the sky together. Dad and I sat there without speaking, trying to forgive her for the torment she was wreaking. It couldn't be undone, so we were seeking to imagine life without her while she was still there, nestled in our arms, her face turned to the sun.

When we went back up, Dad laid Mom on a deck chair and closed her eyes, because they didn't do her any good anymore. He called the doctor in the village, but just for the formalities; he already knew there was nothing anyone could do. They spoke for a long time, but I couldn't hear them; I was watching Mom lying there, her eyes closed, un-weeping, looking like she was peacefully sleeping. Then Dad came to tell me that Mom had drowned because she'd hit her head on a rock, or caught her dress on a log, or some far-fetched thing like that. But I knew perfectly well that you don't swallow a whole bottle of pills to go back to sleep, and then go swim in the deep. I understood: she wanted to go to sleep for good, because sleep was the only zone where her demons left her alone. And she wanted to be at peace all the time, which is no crime. She took those pills of her own free will, and even if I thought it was wrong, I had to go along. I didn't doubt it. Besides, I had no choice about it.

The doctor left Mom with us for one last night, so that we could say good-bye, farewell, adieu, and talk to her a little more. He could see very well that we still had a lot to tell her, that we weren't ready to let her go. So he left instead, after helping Dad lay her on their bed. That was the longest and saddest night of my life, because I didn't know what to tell her, all I knew was that I didn't want to say good-bye. But I stayed anyway, for Dad's sake.

Slumped in my chair, I sat there, watching him talk to her, comb her hair and lay his head on her belly to cry. He scolded her and thanked her, chastised, apologized and criticized, sometimes all in the same sentence. But it made sense, because in just one night, he didn't have time to say things right. He had to cram a lifetime's confabulation into a single conversation.

He was mad at her and at himself, and sad for all three of us. He talked about how our life used to be, and about all the things we wouldn't do, the dances that were through, and even if it sounded confusing, I understood everything he said because I felt the same way, without being able to express it. My words bumped against my closed lips and got stuck in my tightened throat. All I had were morsels of memories jostling each other; nothing could stay long enough to feel whole, because you can't remember an entire life in one night; it's impossible. It's mathematical, as Dad would have said in different circumstances.

And then the sun rose, chasing away the night, and Dad closed the shutters against the light. We both liked being there in the dark with Mom, and wanted it to go on. Neither one of us wanted to greet this new, motherless day, so we closed the shutters to keep it at bay.

In the afternoon, well-dressed men in suits came to pick up Mom's mortal remains. Dad told me they were called undertakers, and their job was to look sad when they came to take dead people away, and to pretend to be in mourning, too. And although I thought that sounded like a strange job, I was still glad to share my sorrow with someone, even for just a moment. There could never be enough people to carry such a heavy load of grief.

They took Mom away, without coffin or bouquet, to wait for the funeral in a special place just for that purpose. Dad explained that you can't keep the dead at home in places that are hot, but I didn't really understand why not. It wasn't as though she could escape, so why all the red tape? We had already kidnapped her once from the loony birds' pen; we weren't going to do it again. I knew there were rules for the living, but it turned out there were rules for the dead, too. Who knew? It was strange, but that's how it was.

To share our sorrow, Dad asked the Creep to take an unscheduled vacation. He got there the very next day, with a cold cigar and clammy skin. He fell into Dad's arms and started sobbing; I'd never seen his shoulders shake like that. He was crying so hard his moustache was covered in snot, and his eyes were a red that was well "beyond reason." He came to share our sorrow, but he brought his own, too, which made a lot of sorrow for one house. To drown it, Dad opened a bottle of a liquid so strong I wouldn't even have poured it on the roots of the tree. Dad let me sniff it, and it burned the hairs in my nose, but they took big swigs of it all day long. I watched them drink and talk and then drink and sing. They only brought up happy memories, so they laughed a lot, and I wound up laughing, too, because you can't be miserable all the time.

Then the Creep fell off his chair like a sack, and Dad fell, too, trying to help him up, because the Creep was a big package that was hard to lift. They laughed out loud, crawling around; Dad was half shaking with belly laughs, half crying real tears, and the Creep was rummaging around with his nose to the floor, like a wild boar, searching for his glasses, which had fallen from his shrimpy ears. I'd never seen anything like it, and when I went to bed, I couldn't help wondering what Mom would have said. Glancing around, I thought I saw her ghost, for a second at the most, sitting on the guardrail and laughing and clapping like crazy.

For the week before the funeral, Dad left me with the Creep all day and watched over me himself at night. During the day, he locked himself inside his study to work on a new book, and at night, he kept me company. He never slept, though he may have wept. He drank cocktails straight from the bottle, smoked his pipe to stay awake, and kept away from the lake. For someone who never went to bed, he seemed neither tired nor unhappy, but focused and joyous instead. He hummed as badly as ever, but like anything that's done cheerfully, it was bearable.

During the day, the Creep and I tried to keep ourselves busy. He took me for walks around the lake, and we had rock-skipping competitions. He spoke humorously about his work at Luxembourg Palace. We played Russian Droolette, but our hearts weren't in it, and everything seemed sad. The walks were always too far, and the rocks didn't skip far enough. The humor wasn't really all that funny, he mostly joked about money, and the almonds and olives always missed their target, or hit us in the face, without laughter as a saving grace. When Dad watched over me at night, he mumbled stories that brought us no delight. Every morning, before the sun was fully up, I'd see him sitting there, on his chair, looking at me with that peculiar gaze that had accompanied all my days.

Spanish cemeteries aren't like regular ones. Instead of suffocating the dead under a huge stone and a ton of dirt, they arrange them neatly in giant cubbyholes with drawers. In the village cemetery, there were rows and rows of cubbyholes, and pine trees to shade them from the summer heat. The dead were put into drawers to make it easier for people to come and see them.

The town priest was there to officiate the ceremony. He looked kind and elegant in his white-and-gold vestments. He had just one long strand of hair that he had wrapped all the way around his head, to try to make it look like he wasn't bald. The strand was so long that it started in the middle of his forehead and went all the way around, winding up tucked behind one ear. Neither the Creep nor Dad nor I had ever seen anything like it.

The men in suits had come with their professional sadness and their big dark car with Mom in her coffin in the trunk. Mademoiselle was there, too; I had draped some black lace around her face. She behaved well and never fell into shrieking or squawking; she kept her beak shut and let the priest do the talking.

When they took Mom out of the hearse to place her in front of her future drawer, it seemed like things couldn't get any worse. But then there was a sudden gust of wind. Above our heads, the pine branches danced and pranced. At first, the priest prayed in Spanish, and we answered in French. But with the wind, his strand of hair kept coming undone, whipping all over the place, looking for fun. Trying to snatch it away from the wind and stick it back behind his ear made him lose his train of thought. He would pray a little, then stop to save his hair from the air, but the strand kept getting stranded. His prayers were all choppy and his skull was blotchy, and we got completely lost in the Mass. Dad leaned toward the Creep and me to whisper that the priest's hair antenna must be tuned toward God usually, but with all that wind, he'd lost his reception and couldn't hear the divine message.

Well after that, it was impossible to keep a straight face. Dad was trying to hold in a self-satisfied grin, because he knew no one else could come up with stories like that. Despite his huge girth, the Creep was shaking with mirth, and a minute later, I followed his lead. Soon we were all doubled over with laughter, trying our best to catch our breath, but we got carried away in a way that was quite unusual for a funeral. The priest was staring at us, with one hand on his head, locking his hair antenna down and blocking out its message from God. But we couldn't stop giggling, and when one of us managed to calm down, he'd catch one of the others' eye and burst out all over again. We were like three silly kids, although the Creep and my dad were grown men. In the end, we had to cover our eyes to keep our faces straight. The priest was dumbstruck, thinking it was just his luck to get stuck preaching to a bunch of lunatics out in the sticks.

When it was time to put Mom into her drawer, we put "Bojangles" on the turntable, and that was a very moving moment. Because the music was like Mom, happy and sad at the same time. "Bojangles" echoed through the cemetery, sounding both mournful and merry. The notes from the piano keys nearly brought us to our knees, but the lyrics whirled and twirled in the air, making us feel like she was still there. The song went on for so long that I had time to see Mom's ghost dancing in the distance and clapping like she used to do. People like that never really die completely, I thought with a smile. I'll see her again in a while. Before we left, Dad unveiled a white-marble plaque on which he'd had engraved, "I will love every woman you have ever been, eternally." And I hadn't added anything, because for once, he had spoken the plain truth.

When I woke up the next morning, Dad wasn't there. The ashtray still had an ember of his sweet pipe tobacco, and the cloud of his smoke was still drifting in the air, but there was no one in his chair. On the terrace, I found the Creep, staring into space, his cigar finally lit. He told me that Dad had dashed off to be with Mom, he'd disappeared into the woods, just before dawn, so that when I awoke, he would already be gone. The Senator said he wasn't coming back, not ever, but I already knew that; the empty chair had told me as much. Now I knew why he had been so focused and happy: he was getting ready to join Mom for a long journey. I couldn't really blame him. That craziness belonged to him, too. It could only exist if they were both there to share it. Now I was going to have to learn to live without them. I was going to find out the answer to a question I had always wondered about: how do other children manage to live without my parents?

Dad had left all his notebooks on his desk. Our whole life was written in them, like a novel. It was truly a marvel, he had caught it all—the ups and downs, the dances and lies, the laughter and tears, the taxes, the Creep, Mademoiselle and the Prussian horseman, Air Bubble and Sven, the abduction and our great escape to the castle in the air—it was all there. He had described Mom's outlandish outfits and outrageous outbursts, her crazy dancing and passion for drinking, her beautiful smile, plump cheeks and long eyelashes fluttering over eyes drunk with joy. Reading his book, I felt like I was reliving the whole thing all over again. Amen.

I called his novel *Waiting for Bojangles*, because we were always waiting for him, and I sent it to a publisher. He told me that it was clever and well written, that he could make neither head nor tails of it, and that that was why he wanted to publish it. So my father's book, with its lies going backward and forward, flew to bookstores around the world. People read *Bojangles* on the beach, in bed, at work, in the metro; whistling as they turned the pages, they laughed and danced with us, cried with Mom and lied with Dad and me, so it was almost as though my parents were still alive. It was kind of far-fetched, but life is often like that, which is fine with me.

12.

"*Look at the chapel, George, it's filled with people praying for us!*" she'd exclaimed in the empty building.

Then, skipping to the central nave, she tied her white shawl over her mane, turning it into a bridal train. Before us was a huge stained-glass window, to which the rising sun had brought a soft, mystical glow. A sudden gust blew dust from the cover of an old psalter, making it whirl and twirl above the altar.

"*I swear before God Almighty, that all the people I will ever be will love you as my husband eternally!*" she intoned, my chin between her hands—the better to hypnotize my enchanted eyes.

"*Before God I swear with all my might, to love all those you will be day and night, to cherish you as my wife, and keep you company throughout your life; I hereby promise that I will always follow, wherever you choose to go,*" I had replied, laying my hand on her face as she grinned with wild abandon.

"Do you swear before all the angels that you will follow me everywhere, really truly everywhere?"

"Yes, everywhere, really truly everywhere!"

About the Author

Olivier Bourdeaut was born in 1980 in a house with no television, so he has been a voracious reader since a very young age. He hesitated for a long time before deciding to write, because he felt so puny compared to the writers on his bookshelf. But a "surge of megalomania" (in his own words) allowed him to finish his first novel, *Waiting for Bojangles*.